O'FEAR

Peter Corris

A Perfect Crime Book

DOUBLEDAY

NEW YORK   LONDON   TORONTO   SYDNEY   AUCKLAND

A PERFECT CRIME BOOK
PUBLISHED BY DOUBLEDAY
a division of Bantam Doubleday Dell Publishing Group, Inc.
666 Fifth Avenue, New York, New York 10103

DOUBLEDAY is a trademark of Doubleday, a division of
Bantam Doubleday Dell Publishing Group, Inc.

All of the characters in this book are fictitious,
and any resemblance to actual persons, living or dead,
is purely coincidental.

BOOK DESIGN BY TASHA HALL

Library of Congress Cataloging-in-Publication Data

Corris, Peter.
O'Fear / by Peter Corris.
p.   cm.
"A Perfect Crime book."
I. Title.
PR9619.3.C595O34   1991
823—dc20   91-12544
                                    CIP
ISBN 0-385-42119-2

November 1991

First Edition in the United States of America

For
Robin and Virginia Wallace-Crabbe

O'FEAR

1

"Did you know a man named Barnes Todd?" Cy Sackville asked me.

"What do you mean, did? I *do* know him. Barnes Todd."

"I'm sorry, Cliff. You don't know him any more. He's dead."

"Shit," I said. "Everybody's dying these days. How come you and I aren't dead, Cy?"

Sackville smiled his expensive lawyer's smile, the one that means we're going to win but it'll cost you. "I keep myself fit and I work in a profession known for the longevity of its members. Whereas you . . ."

"Don't," I said. "On both counts. Well, private eyes live longer on average than some people."

"Who?"

"Astronauts. I'm sorry to hear about Todd. He wasn't that old, was he?"

"About fifty, bit more."

Depressing. But I was determined not to be too depressed,

there had been too much of that in my life recently. "It's always nice to see you, Cy, but why the sudden summons to your pricy presence? You weren't Todd's lawyer, were you?"

Sackville shook his well-groomed head. He's about my age, which is more than forty, and I rate him marginally brighter and about twenty times richer than me. At five foot seven he's six inches shorter, and we both weigh about twelve stone. You can see what a good team we make. "You don't seem very upset at my news."

"I didn't know him *well!*" I snapped.

Sackville raised one eyebrow. He was sitting behind his big polished desk under a painting with a lot of clouds and light in it. It looked as if it could float off the wall any minute. Then it could float out the window, across Martin Place and maybe down the Pitt Street mall. Since the big stock market crash, I had been in a few plush offices where space had opened up on the walls. But Cy has always been careful and patient. "You seem to be under a lot of strain," he said.

Usually Cy's affluence, displayed in the wood panelling of his office and the cut of his suits, amused me; today it got under my skin. I shrugged and plucked at the fabric of the chair I was sitting in. I was pretty sure I could get a finger into the upholstery and do some damage. "I've got a few problems," I said.

"Women?"

"No woman. That's one of the problems."

"Money?"

"Ditto. What's all this about Todd?"

Sackville fiddled with a file on his desk. "It's a bit weird. I got a call from Todd's solicitor, name of Hickie. One-man show in Bondi Junction. Well, it's not a bad location for certain kinds of work. Anyway, Hickie got a letter from Todd a couple of days before his death."

I suppose that's when I took it in properly—that Barnes Todd was dead. I met him almost twenty years ago when I was happily married and looking for a cheap house. He dabbled in real estate, among a lot of other things. He found the Glebe terrace I still lived in, helped with the finance and a few other problems. I'd seen him perhaps two or three times a year since then—at the pub, in the street, or in a restaurant. He was about ten years older than me and he'd served in the Korean war. We used to have a drink and joke about our wars. Mine was the Malayan emergency, which had started earlier than Korea and gone on longer, to 1960. I'd been in on the very end of it. The talk drove Cyn, my then wife, nuts. This was years ago, of course. Until recently, war talk has excluded women in our society. Maybe it's different in the Middle East. Nowadays you can meet female journos and photographers who know a bit about it, but Cyn knew war from books and films, which give you only a shadow of the physical and mental truth. Anyway, I'd liked what I'd seen of Barnes Todd.

The memories didn't improve my mood. "What's this exchange between legal chaps got to do with me?"

"You *are* in a bad way. Have you been playing tennis or doing anything for your body lately?"

"No," I said. "My body's been letting me down. It feels tired in the morning and it won't sleep at night. Get on with it, Cy."

"I had to ascertain that you knew Todd. That you were acquaintances, at least."

"You've done that. He was a big bloke, bald and getting fat. He didn't do much for his body either, but I would've expected it to last him a fair while longer. How did he die?"

"Car accident. He went over a cliff down on the south coast."

I nodded. "He had a house down there, I remember. I used to think he was lucky to have it."

Sackville grunted. He has a house at Palm Beach, so I suppose he doesn't think much of the south coast. "Wife. No children. Have you met his wife, Cliff?"

"No. I thought he was a bachelor with girlfriends. I saw him with a few women over the years. Look, now I come to think of it, I don't think I've seen him for a year or more."

"Hickie tells me he was married about a year ago. To . . . let me see . . ." He opened the file and flicked over a page. "Felicia Armstrong. Younger than him. She's now a fairly rich, fairly young widow."

I dug the finger under the binding on the chair and felt the stitching. It gave a little. "Cy," I said, "get to the point. As far as I know Todd was a good bloke. If I'd heard about it, I'd have gone to his funeral. Maybe. Like I'd go to yours, or Harry Tickener's."

Sackville shuddered. "Don't speak of us in the same breath. Tickener smokes forty Camels a day. It's very likely you'll get the chance to go to his funeral. I plan to outlive you."

"You're risking a violent death by playing the close-mouthed lawyer on me. I could be out making money." I leaned forward and stared at his face. I saw no lines, good teeth, gold frame glasses, and an even tan.

Cy blinked. "I'm glad to see you can still clown. I was beginning to worry about you. You look as if you've just copped a ten-year sentence with no remissions."

I had had a few snorts of mid-morning wine and hadn't stood too close to the shaver. I needed a haircut and my twice-broken nose has wanted straightening for twenty-five years. I let my tainted breath drift across his desk, sniffed loudly, and stroked my stubble like Mickey Rourke. "What's the bottom line, Cy?"

"I remember when you used to play the alcoholic," Sackville said. "After Cyn left you. It went on too long and it wasn't all that convincing, or funny. Barnes Todd has left you some money."

"Why?"

"To find out who murdered him."

I sat back in the chair. Sackville unhooked his glasses and set them down gently on top of the file. He massaged the bridge of his nose and tried to look grave, but there was a flicker of amusement in his eyes. It irritated me, the way a lot of small things had lately. *What's so funny?* I thought. I'd been in this business for nearly fifteen years. I'd found murderers before, hadn't I? Well, stumbled across a couple. "How much money?" I said harshly.

"Ten thousand dollars. His wife's not too happy about it."

2

A rock band was playing in the Martin Place amphitheatre when I left Cy's office. The drummer and the bass guitarist had shaven heads; the singer and lead guitarist had hair to their waists and both wore leather skirts, high-heeled boots, and heavy make-up. I suspected the singer was a man. Twenty years ago they would all have been arrested for creating a public nuisance, but now the shoppers and lunchers walked by or paused to listen while they ate. None was visibly corrupted. The singer screamed, "Fuck me!" into the microphone, but no one did, at least not there and then.

By the time I crossed Castlereagh Street the heavy, jolting music was a thin wail and by Macquarie Street the traffic was making more noise. I'd told Sackville the truth—business was bad and money was short. I bought a sandwich and shared a seat outside the Public Library with a young Japanese couple, clearly tourists, and a woman in a long overcoat who was muttering to herself as she crunched hard frozen peas from a packet. I ate the

sandwich and considered the jottings I had made in my notebook.

I had the addresses and telephone numbers of Michael
Hickie, the lawyer, and Felicia Todd, née Armstrong, the wife.
Barnes Todd had apparently lived in Coogee, which didn't surprise me. I could see him as an ocean-views, early-swimming
type. Hickie's office was in Bondi Junction, which didn't mean
anything in particular. Cy had given me a report on the accident, if that's what it was: Barnes Todd's Holden Calais had
failed to hold the road coming down Bulli Pass at 1 A.M. on 26
January. The car had fallen a long way and hit a lot of trees and
rocks on the way down. It had exploded, and people at first had
taken the noise and fire for a bit of Australia Day whoopee.

I crumpled the sandwich wrapper and bag and tossed them
into a bin. The tourists were bent over a guidebook, talking
intently. The woman in the overcoat had started tossing the peas
to the pigeons, which weren't very interested.

"Bloody pigeons," the woman said, "bloody buggers."

The Japanese man inclined his head politely. "I beg your par-
don?"

The woman looked as if she might shower him with the peas,
so I stood and moved around to block her. "She's talking to the
pigeons," I said. "Don't worry about her. Enjoy your stay."

"Thank you," the man said. "Can you tell us where is Mrs.
Macquarie's chair?"

I gave them directions and explained that it wasn't really a
chair, just a rock.

"This is a very strange country," he said.

The woman with the peas had left the bench and was walking
towards the street, dropping a pea with every step.

"Yes," I said. "It is."

Since the media barons started selling their papers and magazines and TV stations to each other, it's become harder for a
man in my line of work to keep his press contacts in good order.

For years I had relied on my friendship with Harry Tickener to gain access to the resources of the *News*. Now that paper was part of a package that might or might not be traded, and Harry had taken six months' leave while they sorted it out. He was at home writing a book, with his door locked and his answering machine switched on, twenty-four hours a day. So I used the Public Library to check the newspaper reports on Barnes Todd's death.

I had barely glanced at the papers in January. The early weeks had been good or bad for crime, depending on your point of view. There had been several bank robberies and a spectacular payroll grab by seven men with shortened shotguns. That was a lot of firepower, but $1.2 million was a lot of money. Even if I had been reading the papers in my usual inattentive way, I could easily have missed the small item headed " 'Bonfire' a funeral pyre." This wasn't strictly accurate, because Todd had been thrown clear of the car and had died in Wollongong hospital soon after. Otherwise, the details were pretty much as Sackville had stated. Sergeant Anderson of the Bulli police had his say about the dangers of Bulli Pass. The report gave the names of three witnesses—Mr. M. Simpson and Mr. C. Bent had helped to put out the fire started by the exploding car after Mr. W. Bradley had alerted them. I wondered why W. Bradley hadn't fought the flames. "Mr. Todd was alone in the car. He had attended a party in Sydney and was driving to Thirroul to join his wife for a holiday in their beach house." Implication— Barnes Todd had got pissed in the city and wiped himself out in the country. An old story.

I flicked through the pages and found the funeral notice. Private, cremation, no flowers. No suspicious circumstances, no inquest. The accident was almost two months in the past. There was no sign that a man had been murdered except some sort of signal from the man himself. I was intrigued, and there haven't been many days in my life when $10,000 wouldn't have come in handy.

I left the library and walked through the Domain and Wool-loomooloo to my office in Darlinghurst. The morning had been cool with a southerly breeze and clouds banking up to the east; now the sky had cleared and the air was still. It was hot and I carried my jacket over my shoulder. I sweated freely but my wind was good on the upgrades. I wasn't a candidate for the City to Surf, but I'd back myself for two lengths of the Bondi promenade against Cy Sackville any day.

Thoughts of Bondi were much on my mind as I turned into St. Peter's Lane. You hear of people who have lived their whole lives in the one house and you shudder, but right now I was yearning for a little permanency. The building that houses my office was up for renovation. I didn't want to be renovated or to pay a renovated rent. A few of us tenants—such as the painless depilator and the iridologist—had got together and made an approach to the owner. The result had been an avalanche of paper—notices from various bodies declaring the building unsafe and unsanitary, reports indicating how many provisions of the wiring and plumbing regulations were being violated, and the threat of a rent hike anyway. Since then the iridologist had left and my footsteps in the corridors were sounding more and more hollow. I didn't want to move, but I had had a very attractive offer of a place in Hastings Parade, Bondi.

"Afternoon, Cliff. *Love* your hours." The depilator, whose office was next to mine, was a fiftyish woman named Paula. Paula had dyed red hair, scarlet fingernails, and a mouth painted to match. She always wore red clothes and if her throat got cut some day, it would be a while before anyone noticed.

"Don't get the wrong idea. I've been at work all night."

She rubbed hard at the dust on the glass panel in her door with her sleeve, got it satisfyingly dirty, and gave me a broad wink. "That's what I mean, lover."

I blew the dust from the business card that carries my name and is held in place by a drawing pin—my version of the professional nameplate—and bent to pull at a promising-looking envelope. It was stuck under the door. I straightened up, trying not to feel stiff. "Have you got any plans, Paula? About moving?"

"Yeah," she said. "They can pull it down around me. Don't pin your dreams on the fat envelope, Cliff. I got one too. It offers you a chance to win a Fiji island, a stud racehorse, and a speedboat. There's a video of the horse and the boat in action."

"What d'you have to do?"

She snorted. "I didn't bother to find out."

"Maybe I can record over the tape. Get an episode of *Miami Vice.*"

"I wouldn't bet on it. Buggers've probably fixed it so you can't."

I shoved hard and got the door open. The offending envelope was just as Paula had said. To win one of the fabulous prizes you had to invest $10. I put the video cassette on my desk and threw the rest of the information away. There was no other mail, which didn't surprise me. Things have changed in Darlinghurst: the white ants have made a couple of steps on the second flight of stairs hazardous unless you know them, which my clients naturally don't, and Primo Tomasetti has moved his tattooing establishment several blocks away, so I no longer have a parking place. As a result, I've been doing most of my dwindling business from home, where I installed my only hired help—an answering machine.

But you never know; I once had a client who waited for forty-eight hours outside my office to see me. Another time someone left a telephone number and a cheque for a thousand bucks under the door. I wouldn't feel right without an office. I brushed dust from the chair and settled down with the telephone and my notebook. Michael Hickie had a secretary who sounded as if she just loved to answer the phone, take down names and consult her boss's appointments book. So much eagerness is suspicious; when she tried to squeeze me in for tomorrow I suggested later today and she buckled under the pressure. Four-thirty P.M. Maybe Mike and I could commiserate on how slow business was.

The telephone at the Todd residence in Coogee rang for a long time before a woman answered. Deep voice, careful vowels.

"Hello. Felicia Todd speaking."

"Mrs. Todd, my name's Cliff Hardy."

"Oh."

"I was sorry to hear about Barnes. I think we have a few things to discuss."

"Perhaps. Have you spoken to Michael Hickie?"

"I'm seeing him this afternoon."

"Eager, aren't you?"

"I'm sorry. What do you mean?"

"Never mind. I think you should see the solicitor first, then I'll talk to you if it seems necessary."

"Okay," I said. "Will you be at home later this afternoon?"

"Where the hell else would I be?"

She hung up and I put the phone down gently. Grief takes many forms and anger is one of them. I could respect that. Greed is another matter and misanthropy another still. They are harder to deal with. I had time to kill before the appointment in Bondi Junction, and I used it to recall everything I could about Barnes Todd. There wasn't much: he had been a soldier, then he had sold real estate and had an interest in a trucking firm "and other things." I could hear Todd's voice, usually slightly blurred by alcohol, but always cheerful, and he never seemed to big-note himself.

Not that he wasn't aggressive. I could recall a couple of fights and near-fights. On one occasion he flattened a smaller man and apologised immediately. He seemed to have a healthy appetite for life. He'd travelled a bit and said he planned to do more. I tried to remember the names of the women I'd seen him with, and couldn't. They had been varied—some particularly good-looking and not particularly bright, others vice versa. Todd seemed to find them all amusing. I tried to recall Cyn's attitude to him but that was confusing. I had an idea she wasn't too keen on him but it might just have been me she didn't care for.

3

Paying at the car park led me to think about how my fee for this case might be handled. Would it be money up front, or a version of my usual $175 a day, plus expenses? Or payment only for results? That could be tricky. I wasn't even sure it would be legal. I drove along Oxford Street and onto the short stretch of freeway that runs beside Centennial Park and out to the eastern suburbs. In just a couple of hours the clouds were back. They hung dark and heavy over the high glittering buildings of Bondi Junction to the right of the freeway, as if they were going to press them down to join the surrounding, unimpressive landscape.

I beat another Falcon, a newer one than mine, into a parking place near the bus depot. The driver shrugged and cruised on: we Falcon men are a laidback lot. I was wearing my jacket again and had tucked my shirt in neatly and finger-combed my hair when I presented myself to Hickie's secretary. She wasn't impressed—probably the crumpled pants and the stubble. She pointed at a narrow door to the right of her desk.

"Mr. Hickie will be free in a few minutes, Mr. Hardy. If you'd like to take a seat?"

The office was bright and freshly painted, but small. The secretary hardly had space for her chair and desk, and the seat I took couldn't have been more than six feet from her elbow. She pecked at her typewriter.

"Busy?" I said.

She smiled brightly. "Oh, yes." She was young and pretty with a lot of dark hair pulled back and a neat dress. At a guess it was her first job. It might have been Hickie's first office too; the copies of *Time* and the *Bulletin* didn't go back beyond the previous June. Ah, that Hardy, always detecting. After ten minutes and about twenty words on the typewriter, the door opened inwards and a man appeared in the narrow space. The typewriter went click, click, click, rapidly.

"Mr. Hardy?" Hickie gestured for me to stand and enter. It was a constrained gesture because he didn't have much room to make it in. I stepped past him into a room that might have been larger than the outer one, but not by much. Hickie was a medium-sized man wearing a white shirt, striped tie, and the vest and trousers of a three-piece suit. The coat hung on the back of his chair and was crushed flat at the collar where he had leaned against it. He wasn't as young as I'd guessed, about thirty. He had plenty of brown hair and was good-looking enough not to have to worry about it. Intelligence and anxiety warred in his features.

I shook his extended hand and he waved me into a chair. If I had turned the chair around and stuck my legs out I could probably have put my feet on the bookcase that held his legal texts. He went behind his desk, sat down, and did some more suit coat crushing.

"Cy Sackville gave me your number," I said. "And some details. I'd be grateful for a few more."

"I imagine you would. It's a curious bit of business."

I jerked my thumb over my shoulder at the bookcase. "Not much about it in those."

He smiled. "That's right. Sorry to be so formal about it, but could I see some identification?"

I handed over my enquiry agent licence, which carries an unflattering photo. He scrutinised it closely, looked at me, and handed it back.

"Thanks. Sackville spoke very highly of you. He said you'd had some legal training."

"He's being ironic. He probably means time spent being questioned by the cops. I wouldn't call what I had training. I did a couple of years of law. Failed Contract, disliked Torts."

He grimaced. "Failed a few myself along the way. Took me longer to get the degree than it should have."

"I'd never have got it."

"Neither would I, probably, without Barnes Todd."

"Ah."

He unbuttoned his shirt cuffs and rolled them back to show thick, strong forearms that had done some hard work in their time. "I haven't been in practice long, as you can probably see. I'm making ends meet, but it's going to be harder without Barnes."

I nodded. I've never minded the autobiographical approach to a subject.

"I worked for him, in the holidays and when I had to go part-time to earn money. Truck driving. He was a great bloke. Gave me a lot of help and encouragement."

"And his business."

"Yes. After I qualified."

Hickie seemed anxious to talk, but you can never tell with lawyers. They're likely to clam up at any moment, especially if you get pushy. "I want to ask a lot of questions," I said. "You'll have to tell me when to stop."

"Sure."

"Was Todd doing well financially?"

"He certainly was. And getting better all the time. He was expanding. Leasing property, developing. He was going into storage in a big way—that's a coming thing. So I was handling contracts, conveyancing, a few court actions. A few problems came up, but we got along . . ."

I held up my hand. "I wasn't accusing you of murdering him, Mr. Hickie."

He looked offended. "What? Oh, I get it. Well, I didn't mean to sound defensive. It's just that I've lost the man who put me on my feet personally, you understand? Also a friend and a client and a business associate."

"You were involved with him in a business sense?"

"Just in a small way. But it might've grown into something bigger. It still might, if Felicia wants to keep Barnes Enterprises running."

"We'll get to her in a minute. What can you tell me about this bequest to me? This investigate-his-murder thing?"

"I drew up Barnes' will. Or re-drew it. There's nothing remarkable about it. His estate goes to Felicia. There's a couple of bequests to employees and friends. At the risk of sounding defensive again, I'll say there's no bequest to me."

"When was this will drawn?"

"About a year ago. It was one of the first things I did for him. And he'd only got married a few months before that, so the timing was right for everyone."

The storm that had been gathering broke just then. Rain lashed the window and the light in the room dropped suddenly. Hickie was deep in his story and didn't seem to notice.

"I got a letter from him a day before he died. He told me to set aside ten thousand for you to find out who killed him if he died suddenly."

"Have you got the letter?"

"Yes, but I can't show it to you. Felicia's considering challenging it. All documents are private until she decides."

I grinned at him. "C'mon, Michael. As one battler to another. Let's see the copy."

He opened a drawer in his desk, took out a folder, and extracted a photocopied sheet. He passed it to me. I squinted at it in the gloom and he got up to turn on the overhead light. The date was 24 January; the letterhead was Barnes Enterprises with an address in Botany. The handwritten message was simple:

Dear Michael,

If I disappear or get shot or have what's called an accident, I want you to allot ten thousand dollars from my estate to a private investigator by the name of Cliff Hardy to look into the circumstances. Give Hardy any and all help you can. This could be a false alarm. Hope to see you soon but if not, good luck.

The note was signed, "B.T."

"You can keep it," Hickie said. "I've got the original and other copies."

I folded the paper and put it in my pocket. A tap came at the door and the secretary poked her head through.

"I'm about to go, Mr. Hickie. Is there anything . . . ?"

Hickie shook his head. "No thanks, Jenny. See you tomorrow. Good night."

"Things are slack," I said after Jenny had gone.

Hickie sighed. "Yeah. I hope I can pay Jenny's wages next week. It'd help if Felicia could make up her mind about a few things."

"Do you think Barnes Todd was murdered?"

"I don't know."

"Was he doing anything that could've got him killed?"

"He was making money."

"And enemies?"

He shrugged. "Don't they go together?"

"I'll need your co-operation," I said. "I'll have to know everything about his business dealings, new and old."

"Happy to help. But you'll have to get past Felicia first. She could hold up settling the estate for a hell of a long time if she wanted to."

"I've got an appointment to see her tonight."

"Good." He looked out the window and noticed the rain. "Shit," he said. "My car's in dock."

"Where d'you live?"

"Randwick."

"I'm going to Coogee, I'll drop you."

We got moderately wet running through the rain to the car. On the drive to Randwick, Hickie seemed tense. We passed a pub and he said: "I used to drink in there with Barnes."

"He was a good drinker, as I recall."

"He used to be before he met Felicia. She put him on a diet. He lost weight. Slept well. Looked years younger."

"When did you last see him?"

"I looked it up. It was five weeks before his death. I used to see him more often than that, but we met less and less after he got married."

There was an edge to his voice but whether it applied to the marriage or the wife I couldn't tell. "What's she like? What should I take—flowers, Perrier?"

"Just take your wits with you. She does Mensa puzzles for fun."

"She sounded pretty emotional on the phone."

Hickie nodded. "That too," he said.

4

The rain had eased to a drizzle and the light had improved by the time I dropped Hickie at a neat semi in a quiet Randwick street. When he opened the front door an Old English sheepdog broke free and bounded to the gate. It bounced there, barking and looking back at Hickie. It's hard to have any negative feelings about a man who takes his dog for walks. Hickie was looking more solid and reliable by the minute. I mimed the action of telephoning and he nodded. I waved and drove off in the direction of Coogee.

It was a little after six o'clock, which is a difficult time to go calling on people. Some are settling down to the news or the soaps on TV, others are having a quiet drink or several. It's not a companionable time, and I wasn't feeling very companionable myself. As I made the turn into Coogee Bay Road I remembered that Helen Broadway had looked at a few places in Coogee before settling on her flat in Tamarama. I'd had good times with Helen, perhaps better than with any other woman, and then bad times. It was still hard to accept, but I hadn't seen her in more than a year, and for all I knew she might be pregnant again or running Radio Kempsey.

Felicia Todd's house was at the end of a street that led directly to the beach. It was on a corner, a long, low structure that faced north, but the eastern side had been opened out with french windows and a courtyard to give it an effective face to the water. You can almost feel the sand under the tar and grass in parts of Coogee. I'd heard of houses in this area which were sliding to the sea as the ancient dunes moved under them, but this place looked rock-solid: light-coloured bricks, sandstone foundations, slate roof, deep garden front and back—big money. It and the one next door were among the few houses in the street, which was dominated by middling-sized blocks of flats.

I parked opposite and looked the place over. It was set high up on the block with no space for a driveway or garage. So one of the few cars parked in the street was probably hers. So what? I was wasting time. I wished I'd stopped for a drink on the way. Hickie had said a keen mind was a necessity for dealing with Mrs. Todd, and mine was often keener for a little oiling. Sitting there with the light grey sea spread out in front of me and the day dying in the west, I realised that I was out of practice. I'd talked to two lawyers today, and that was fine. That wasn't so far from the work I'd been doing lately—bodyguarding nervous businessmen, minding money and even, God help me, serving summonses. But this was different. This was a call on a private citizen who had experienced grief. Maybe I'd be just one more little bit of grief to her. No help at all. A tough row to hoe. I like to think of myself as helpful.

I scuttled through the drizzle across the street, through the gate, and up the flagstoned path and a steep set of wooden steps to the front of the house. Some tall shrubs in the garden dripped water on me. Before I could knock on the door, it opened.

"Mr. Hardy?"

She was just a shape in the half light. A narrow shape with a voice that was low and breathy, like a deep note on a flute. I wasn't ready for the voice. The telephone had flattened out its extraordinary quality.

"Yes, Mrs. Todd?" I had my licence ready for display in my hand, complete with water droplets, but she ignored it.

"I saw you sitting in your car. What were you thinking?"

I gulped and felt stupid. "About the sand dunes of Coogee, or something like that. Among other things."

"A disordered mind," she said. "I should have expected it. You'd better come in."

She pushed out the screen door and stepped back. I followed her down a hallway, with several rooms off to either side, to a galley kitchen and eating area that ran across the whole width of the back of the house. The floorboards were dark and polished; the furniture was old, well cared-for, and functional. There was a sort of butcher's block and bench dividing the kitchen from the eating and sitting space. A large dining table had six chairs drawn up to it, and room for a few more. A pale light that would only last a few minutes more leaked in from the french windows.

She pointed to a cane chair near the window and strode to a sideboard. "Do you drink?"

"Yes," I said.

"Thank God. What?"

"Almost anything that isn't sweet."

She poured hefty measures of a pale liquid into glass tumblers and held one out to me. "Sit down."

I took the chair she had pointed to. Anyone in his right mind would. She dragged one of the chairs away from the table and sat a few feet from me. I sipped the very dry sherry. "Thank you," I said, "that's a very civilised drink."

"Civilisation's overvalued." She smiled as she spoke and took a swig from her glass. She had light brown hair, straight and shoul-

der length. She wore a plain blue dress with a few pleats above
and below the waist. "That's a bit pompous, don't you think?"

"A bit," I said.

Her smile broadened. Her eyes were brown and there was
nothing special about her face. Her features were regular and
pleasing enough but I had the feeling that she could look beautiful in certain moods, or ugly. "Well, Mr. Hardy. Tell me why I
should give you ten thousand dollars."

"Is that the way you see it, Mrs. Todd?"

"Give me another way to look at it."

"To fulfil your late husband's wish."

She grunted and sipped her sherry. "Barnes retained a lot of
false ideas from his past. Macho fantasies about men standing
alone against the odds. I imagine you run on that sort of fuel
too."

I realised I was still holding my licence folder. I shoved it into
my pocket and drank some more sherry, which was warming and
encouraging. If she wanted to spar over sherry, fine. "Not very
much. I take jobs, try to see them through to a reasonable con-
clusion. I know when to stick and when to bail out. Do you think
Barnes' feeling that he might meet with an accident was a fantasy? He didn't strike me as a fantasist."

"How well did you know him?"

Her interrogative style irritated me, like when a sparring partner presses too hard. I was tempted to tell her that I'd known
him longer than she had, and had shared experiences with him
that went pretty deep. But somehow I got the feeling that she'd
have a quick comeback and that I'd lose more ground than I
would win. And I was here to win ground. I told her about my
acquaintanceship with Barnes.

She nodded; the shiny brown hair bounced on her shoulders.
"From his boozy days. When his mind was clouded."

I took a big gulp of the sherry and tried not to say anything
too rude. She was a recent widow after all, even if she seemed to

be handling it pretty well. "You're right up to a point," I said. "I only ever saw him in public places or in his office. We weren't close but he did me a very good turn and if I could have repaid it when he was alive I would have. He never asked me for anything. Not a thing. I'm flattered that he thought well enough of me to write that note to Michael Hickie."

"Michael's a nice young man," she said.

"I'm not as young and not as nice. But I'd still like to repay the favour."

"Would you do it without the money?"

I shook my head. "It'll take a lot of work—a lot of checking and talking to people and getting the runaround. I couldn't afford to do it for free."

"Honest and energetic. Good." She drained her glass and put it on the floor. I got the feeling there wasn't going to be any more sherry so I nursed the inch I had left.

She pushed back her hair and stood. The light had faded almost to nothing and she suddenly looked dark and widowlike. Her low-heeled shoes were dark, like her stockings and dress. She was a bit below average height and slim, but there was a force in the way the dark shape moved towards the passageway. For a moment I thought she was giving me my marching orders and I stirred, but she flicked her fingers at me. "Stay there. I want to show you something."

She walked away and I asserted myself by getting up and pouring another belt of the dry sherry. It was sitting warmly inside my empty stomach and, if it wasn't sharpening my wits, it was making the rest of me feel comfortable. I turned on a light and the room filled with a soft glow that touched the polished wood and the clean glass and metal surfaces. Barnes Todd had left some pretty good animate and inanimate objects behind. I was suddenly aware of another tack to take with the widow.

She came back carrying a stack of enlarged photographs and two framed objects. When she arranged the stuff on the table I saw that one of the framed works was also a photograph. It was a picture of Barnes Todd looking as I had never seen him. His face was much thinner and tanned; his straggly, thinning hair had been clipped away almost to nothing, giving him a hard-edged, no-time-for-that-hair-nonsense look. He was wearing jeans and a loose, dirty sweater and his smile was surprised, spontaneous. He'd just turned away from something I couldn't make out with the light on the glass. I moved my head and looked closer—an easel. And the smears on the sweater were paint.

"He looks great," I said. "Happy inside and out."

"He was." She moved a photograph and the painting to where I could see them better. The photo was of Bondi Beach, but I'd never seen it looking like that. The photo had been taken at dawn; it was overcast, with the horizon and the sea blurred; there appeared to be a mist and an impression that the sea was rising up to envelop the land. The painting was a version of the same thing. It was mostly in blue and white, but it lacked the devastating, visionary quality of the photograph. I admired both, but the photograph said more to me and held my eye.

"Christ. They're good."

"Aren't they?" Her voice was full of pride. "He was an exceptionally talented man. Have a look at these."

The photographs all had the same alarming originality. They were of buildings, the sea and the rocks, some with people and some without. The images seemed to blend so that the people became part of the physical world around them in a way I'd never seen. Some exhibited these qualities more strongly than others. I was reminded of photographs of Aborigines taken by the early missionaries; in them, the blacks stand and sit and the country around them seems to stand and sit in the same attitude. Barnes Todd's photographs were urban versions of the same thing. I stared at them and shook my head. It seemed a fair bet that if he had been able to put these things on canvas the art world would have had to sit up straight.

"What comes to your mind when you look at them?" Felicia Todd said. "What words?"

I was bowled over, but I still had business to conduct. I drank some sherry and turned away from the art display to look at her. "I'm a mug when it comes to pictures. Words? Drysdale, visions and dreams. Also original, if that makes any sense."

"Yes, it does." She collected the photographs and laid them down with their white backs and pencilled inscriptions showing over the painting and the shot of Todd. She was like a magician manipulating the illusions—now you see them and admire, now you don't. "I met Barnes at the State Gallery. I'd gone along to see the Archibald entrants. Didn't know he was interested in art, did you?"

I shook my head.

"And photography?"

"No."

"He was. Always had been. But war and booze and women and business had diverted him from it. He had a vocation, but he'd lost his faith."

"And you were his redeemer."

She snorted. "Sorry. That sounded very prissy. No, it was all secular. I was a good swimmer when I was young. Later, I was a good photographer and a fair painter. I had a gallery once but I was a lousy businesswoman and I lost it. Barnes was great at business, and you can see what he could do with a camera and a brush. I got him swimming three miles a day."

She picked up her empty glass and for a minute I thought it was self-pity time, but she stalked across the room to the sink and filled the glass with water. When she got back, she was composed. For no good reason I thought of the kids' game where you put your hands behind your back and produce scissors, rock, or paper. My bet was that Felicia Todd would do rock nine times out of ten. "I see you got yourself another sherry. How's your liver?"

"Okay. I don't drink as much as I used to. How was Barnes in that way?"

"Getting more civilised. Oh, shit. I just said that was over-valued, didn't I?" She smiled and her whole face seemed to lift and catch the light. She had good cheekbones. Some fine down along her jaw showed in the light giving her a softer, more strokable look. I wondered if Barnes had got around to painting her.

"Did he ever paint you?"

She shook her head. "He said he wasn't ready. God, I didn't want to get into this. I thought you'd be some grasping thug who'd settle for a thousand and go away."

"I won't. I want to know what happened to him."

She looked at me and didn't speak for a long time. When she did her voice seemed to be coming from a long way off. "He sold a few paintings. He was getting an exhibition together, but he wanted to stay in business for a bit longer to finance a real throw at being a painter."

I nodded. "That makes sense. Did he talk to you much about his business?"

"Not a lot. I got some idea of it. I know he had plans to expand but that there was some pretty tough competition. He used to say that trucking and flogging pictures weren't all that different."

"What did he mean?"

"He didn't get on with the gallery owners. Some of them actually threatened him. He laughed about that. I suppose he made enemies. They must have seen what he could be worth."

"Are you saying someone in the art world could have killed him?"

"A dead genius is worth more than a live one."

"Come on."

"Don't sound so surprised. It's a dirty world, believe me. The people who run it are greedy, snobbish crooks."

I knew what she was talking about. "I had a bit to do with it once, but from the other end—forgeries. Did he do enough work for an exhibition?"

"Certainly. I had a break-in a week or so ago. Someone tried to steal the lot. I've moved it since."

"You've got a good alarm system here. I noticed it before."

She nodded. "It worked. You should say, 'You owe it to him to find out what happened. You need help, Mrs. Todd.' "

We were standing by the table; in her low shoes her head came to just above the level of my shoulder. I was behind her: the light threw our shadows forward onto the wall, long thin shadows, close together, almost the same length.

"You owe it to him to find out what happened. You need help, Mrs. Todd."

"Yes," she said. "I do."

5

Felicia Todd heard my stomach rumbling. She laughed and offered to make a herb omelette. I accepted. She also made conversation about a range of subjects as she was cooking and as I
was hunting for plates and forks. I told her what Michael Hickie
had said about her doing Mensa puzzles, and she smiled.

"That was just a joke. Barnes and I were having him on. I'd
looked up the answers."

"It impressed Michael."

"Michael's easily impressed."

"He made a good impression on me. I think he's honest and
has your interests at heart. And his own, of course. He doesn't
want to work out of that little office for the rest of his life. Can't
blame him for that."

"No. I think he has a future. Has he still got that pretty
secretary?"

"Yes, but I think she's hanging by a thread. I know the signs. I had a secretary once, then I had to put her on part-time and then . . ." I mimed a wave goodbye.

"What sort of an office do you work out of now, Cliff?"

We were Cliff and Fel by this time. I told her about the St. Peter's Lane situation and the Glebe situation, which is, essentially, that the house needs repair but is worth a lot of money as it stands. "I've got an offer of a place in Hastings Parade, in Bondi. A lot of my business is in the eastern suburbs anyway. I could combine the house and office and have a better water view."

She shoved the pan under the griller. "Have you got a water view now?"

I put plates on the bench near the oven and took the forks across to the table, also the salt and pepper and some crumpled paper napkins. "Blackwattle Bay," I said. "If I stand on the fence." I pointed out the window to where the ocean was a dark rippling mass, white-flecked and stretching away forever. "Nothing like this."

She pulled the deep pan out; the omelette had risen to the full height of its sides. "This costs, but it's worth the money."

Over the meal we talked mostly about Barnes but some about her. She was thirty-five, born and raised in the Blue Mountains. Dux of Katoomba high school and runner-up in the under-eighteen New South Wales 100 and 200 metres freestyle in 1970. She studied Fine Arts at Sydney University for three years before switching to an art course at Sydney Technical College.

"That's a big switch," I said. "Must've shocked the professors."

"It did. They had me lined up to do a PhD on Gainsborough and the pastoral tradition. I preferred Frida Kahlo, but there was no interest in her. Do you know about her?"

"I saw a programme on television," I said. "Mexican. Tortured stuff."

"Right. I've got a back problem that comes from weight training for swimming. It's nothing like the agony she suffered after her accident, but it's pretty bad sometimes. I related to her and I wanted to learn how to *do*, not teach. Understand?"

"I think so. I'm a practical man myself."

She finished the art course, painted, had no success, inherited some money, and opened a gallery to display adventurous work. "Not mine," she said. "I wasn't ready. I was still scraping them off and doing them again."

I thought of the early cases I'd had; the ones where I muddled through, missed things, half got there. Our plates were empty by this time; we had finished off the French bread and were slicing bad bits from a few elderly pieces of fruit with the knives we had already used.

"Sorry," she said. "I'm a lousy housekeeper."

"So am I," I said. "I call a plate you can brush the crumbs off clean. If they stick, it's dirty."

She laughed. "If I'd met Barnes a few years earlier, I probably wouldn't have lost the gallery. I just didn't know how to do things right, moneywise. D'you want some coffee? You look as if you need it. Were you up all night?"

"No. Why?"

She plucked at her chin and I laughed. "Just careless shaving. Coffee'd be good." I followed her across to the kitchen and rinsed the plates. We hadn't drunk anything with the food and I really wanted the coffee. She put a kettle on the gas, spooned coffee into a glass pot, and set the plunger.

"No milk," she said. "I've neglected the shopping."

"What *have* you been doing?"

"Reading. Going for walks. Feeling randy. We had a great sex life, Barnes and me."

We went back to the table and sat quietly over the black, bitter coffee, looking out at the sea. In the old days, I would have smoked and told myself the ritual and the nicotine stimulated thought. Now I just stared across the road and the randomly parked cars, past the stained concrete buildings and the faded brick ones, to the water. It was the sort of view that was desolate but could be comforting and warming if you had someone to share it with.

"So, d'you want me to look into it, Fel?" I said.

"What does it involve?"

"Raking things up. Talking to people about things they don't want to talk about." I drew a deep breath. "Like this. Was Barnes faithful to you? Were there any other women? Could he have got out of his depth? You must know that he used to hang around with some . . ."

"Glamorous women," she said. "I know I'm not glamorous."

We had stopped sparring long ago, but I felt I was on the ropes again. "I didn't mean anything like that. Glamour mostly just scrapes off. But . . ."

"Men are attracted to it. Active, successful men in particular. No, I'm sure Barnes had given that life away. I expect he would've painted it, later."

"Mm. Well, you seem to be able to handle that side of things. What about the implication in the news story that he was drunk?" This was the line I had been saving and I watched her closely to get her reaction.

She brushed back her hair; it was a plain, forthright gesture but it did good things to her face. "No chance. He wouldn't have had more than a couple of light beers at that party, or a glass of wine. Two at the most. It wasn't a problem for him."

"I'll have to talk to everyone who was there. Ask. Insinuate."

"Sure."

"Fel, I have to ask you about the hospital. You saw him before he died?"

She nodded. She wasn't going to make it easy for me.

"Spoke with him?"

"Yes."

"What did he say?"

"Not much. He was terribly badly injured. He barely had the breath to speak."

"Was his mind clear?"

"I hope not. He'd have been in terrible pain if it was." She sipped at the cold dregs of her coffee. "They rang me at the beach house from the hospital. I suppose it was about two A.M. I drove straight in. They'd been going to operate but they decided there was no point, so I knew he was going to die when I went in to see him. Have you ever talked to a dying person?"

"Yes. Not someone I loved, though."

"We'd talked so much in the time we'd been together . . . stayed up all night talking sometimes, and now there was nothing to say. I couldn't tell him to fight or anything. It was hopeless. He was all broken inside. I just held his hand, really, and waited."

"But he did speak. What did he say?"

"He said . . ." Her voice caught. For a moment I thought all the careful control was about to rupture and spill, but she put the coffee mug on the table and laced her fingers together. "He said, 'Oh, oh, oh,' like that and then a word I don't think I understood."

"What word?"

"It sounded like 'fear,' but I don't think it could have been. I mean, I doubt that he knew what was happening to him. And Barnes wouldn't talk about fear. He knew me, knew who I was. But he just made these sounds and then he gave a sort of shudder and he was gone."

I mouthed the sounds, imitating her deep tone. "Oh, oh . . . oh . . . fear."

She nodded. "Yes. Like that."

"O'Fear," I said. "I understand."

"I don't," she said. "What?"

"It's a man's name, or a sort of nickname. Kevin O'Fearna his name is, but he's called O'Fear. I didn't know Barnes knew him, but he could have. They'd be much the same age and O'Fear's been around. Come to think of it, I believe he was in Korea."

"That again. Bloody Korea, I don't like to think that he was meandering on about that bloody shambles."

The female view of war again. It looked as if Barnes Todd and I had had some marital as well as war experience in common. But it was a side issue now. I shook my head. "I doubt it. He left the note for Michael Hickie about me and then he mentioned O'Fear. There has to be some kind of connection."

"You mean this O'Fear could have . . . killed him?"

"No, no. O'Fear's not a killer. Barnes could have meant that he knows something, or could help in some way."

"You evidently know him, Cliff. Would he help?"

"O'Fear's a funny bloke. He might help you for the price of a drink or he might not even if you offered him a thousand bucks."

"Will you ask him?"

"There's a snag."

"What?"

"The last I heard, O'Fear was in gaol."

6

I left Felicia Todd's house shortly after ten o'clock. I was utterly sober, intrigued by the circumstances surrounding her husband's death and stimulated by her company. She explained that it was grief and loss that had caused her initially to take such a negative attitude to Michael Hickie and Todd's note about me. She was still grieving, but she was ready to go on with her life. I persuaded her to call Hickie and discuss the future of Barnes Enterprises with him. I didn't have to persuade her about the investigation—now she was all for it.

"If he was killed by someone connected with the galleries, I want revenge," she had said. "If it was to do with his business, it should be exposed, shouldn't it? And if it was just an accident, I want to know."

It was a firm enough foundation for me, firmer than some I had worked from. I told her that I'd use the tried and trusted techniques of my semi-profession—badger people in their houses and offices, knock on doors, and use the telephone.

"Good," she said. "What about O'Fear?"

I was thinking about O'Fear as I drove back to Glebe. The rain had set in again and the rhythmic swish of the windscreen wipers helped memory and thought. Kevin O'Fearna had been born in Australia of Irish parents. I remember him telling me that he was distantly related to Gene Tunney, the heavyweight who had beaten Jack Dempsey and earned a fortune and the hatred of a generation of American sports fans. O'Fear had worked as a builder's labourer and sung Irish songs on the Sydney folkie circuit in the 1960s. He made a record that no one bought and went "back" to Ireland for ten years, where he expanded his repertoire, deepened his thirst for Guinness and became more Irish in accent and manner than the Clancy Brothers.

Back in Sydney in the cynical 1980s, living in Glebe where he had always lived, he had done more labouring than singing and, possibly, more drinking than either. He served a term on the Leichhardt Council as a radical environmentalist, which brought him into contact, mostly antagonistic, with union bosses, businessmen, and politicians. He had a son by one of his many women. *Danny O'Fearna must be almost thirty by now, poor devil*, I thought. Danny was a trial to his father, often in trouble with the police. Common opinion was that he was "touched" or "a bit slow."

On the extreme militant wing of the Building Trades Union, O'Fear had been involved in a number of confrontations with heavies hired by the employers, as well as with the police. His adversaries had never heard of Gene Tunney or Joe Hill or Ewan MacColl or any of O'Fear's heroes. Only a week or so ago I'd heard in the Toxteth Arms, one of his favourite watering holes where the Guinness was on tap, that O'Fear had taken on the cops and the bosses and was on remand in Long Bay for trespass and assault.

I became aware of the tail when I made a late turn into

Foveaux Street, Surry Hills. The car behind me slewed a bit as it turned, and its lights flashed in my rear vision mirror. It followed me along Eddy Avenue and up beside the railway. In better-lit Broadway, it dropped back professionally, but I got a good look at it—a dark sedan, Japanese. I got an impression of the licence number—K something M, 2s and a 3, or maybe 3s and a 2. I signalled, maybe a fraction early, and took the turn into Glebe Point Road. *Come on, baby,* I thought. *Come on down to where it's dark, and we can have a chat.* I glanced in the mirror again before the first set of lights, and that was a mistake. The driver must have realised that I was onto him. Instead of following me down to Bridge Road, he swung left into St John's Road. I swore and nearly hit a bus by turning abruptly right. I went down the hill until it was clear behind me and U-turned in front of a truck climbing slowly towards the intersection. I turned left against the red light, burned up to the St John's Road crossing, went right, and hit sixty on the straight stretch to Ross Street. No dark sedan; no Ks, Ms, 2s, or 3s.

Great work, Cliff, I thought. *You signalled too early and looked when you shouldn't have.* It was the sort of sloppy behaviour that got you hurt in the streets these days. In Malaya, it got you killed. The guerrillas could read a lot into a dropped cigarette butt or a broken bootlace. You gave them nothing because it might cost your life. I remembered Barnes Todd saying it was the same in Korea, except that there it was marks in the snow you avoided, or signs that the oil in your Sten gun had iced up. Suddenly, I felt tired. The adrenalin that had flowed when I picked up the tail had burned out, leaving me disappointed, drained, and weary. I drove to my house, which the real estate men have told me is "in demand despite its condition." I felt more or less the same.

The cat upped and left some time back, due, no doubt, to the irregularity of its feeding. I missed it but hadn't got around to getting a replacement. Nor had I resolved the question of regular feeding—why wouldn't the next cat do the same? Of course, if I moved office and house to Bondi there wouldn't be so much of a problem. If you lived where you worked a cat could be fed that much more often. It was something to consider, but not much. No mail through the slot. I walked from the front of the house to the back, ignoring the soft spot in the floorboards two paces from the kitchen. The answering machine light was a steady glow—no calls. The radio I've taken to leaving on when I'm out, more so I won't come back to a dead quiet house than for security reasons, was playing some soft postwar jazz. I twisted the dial savagely until I found some rock. *I'm not a bloody pensioner yet.*

Under the shower I noticed that the mould was doing well in the bathroom and that the fibro strips holding the roof up were sagging. "That'd be white ants," the agent would say. "Big money to fix that, Mr. Hardy."

Big money I didn't have, yet. And with back taxes and a Bankcard account that walked the "credit available" line like a tightrope, there wouldn't be a hell of a lot left of the ten thousand, if I could earn it. I dried off, put on my towelling dressing gown that is shading down from white to grey, and tapped the flagon in the fridge. I sat with the wine and my notebook intending to review what I had on the Todd matter, but other thoughts crowded the case out.

Money and love are the great subjects for reverie; love and money. I remembered the big cheque Peter January had given me after I'd saved his neck and protected his political arse. I had had thoughts of buying land in Kempsey, near Helen Broadway's husband's property. After that idea went bust, I was going to open an office in Southport and live in Byron Bay with Helen and Verity, her daughter. That went bust too. The money ebbed away in airfares and payments to lawyers and champagne and nights in the Hilton.

The love seeped out through the cracks opened up by late-night phone calls, midday telegrams and subterfuges—my sly drinking sessions with Frank Parker and Harry Tickener; Helen's secret notes to Michael, her husband, and extravagant gifts to Verity. In the end, we had nothing to say to each other that wasn't tainted by the experience we'd been through—the lies and deceptions and broken promises. In the end we didn't even say goodbye. She left and I tidied up in her wake. I did a good job on the surface things—the Tamarama flat, the Honda Civic, the books left behind—but I had the feeling I'd be tidying up after her for the rest of my life.

If I wanted it to be that way. I didn't. I swigged some wine and jerked my mind back onto the tracks left by Barnes Todd. I tried to think of him as a soldier, slogging through hostile country, surrounded by enemies, with a limited supply of ammunition but with an objective in mind. I needed to know the objective to gauge the true nature of the threat . . .

The words "break-in" were scribbled on my pad. "Christ," I said aloud. "Whoever tailed me must have picked me up in Coogee."

I scrabbled through the notebook for Felicia Todd's number. It was after midnight, but that hour means nothing to a true watcher. I dialled the number and the phone rang only twice before she picked it up.

"This is Hardy," I said. "I want you to have a look out into the street. See if there's a car parked within watching distance." I gave her the description of the car and the approximation of its licence plate.

She was back on the line quickly, but not too quickly. "No," she said. "The street's clear. That is, I can identify the cars I can see. The flats've got garages. We're . . . I'm an exception. You sound pretty tense, Cliff. What's wrong?"

"I was followed. Probably picked up at your place. A dark sedan—a Datsun or a Toyota. You're sure there's no sign of it?"

"No sign. Look, Cliff, the dog next door howls like a banshee if anyone comes within reach of these houses. And the police've been doing a special patrol since I reported the break-in. Barnes and the local sergeant were on good terms. They went swimming together in the mornings."

I grunted. "Is there anywhere else you can go?"

"Yes. There's our studio."

"Do you go there much?"

"Only once since Barnes died. Why?"

I wanted to know the address, whether it was where she had put Barnes' paintings, whether it had a phone and a bed, but I didn't ask. I had given her my card. Now I told her to call me from a public phone in the morning.

"You think I'm being bugged?"

"I don't know."

"Around ten?"

"Yes."

"I will." There was a pause so long that I thought she might have hung up. Then she said, "I enjoyed it tonight. That sounds terrible, given what we had to talk about. But I did."

"So did I. Take another look for the car."

She was away briefly. "Nothing," she said.

"Good," I said. "Talk to you in the morning, Fel. 'Night."

I made lists of things to do as I finished the wine: talk to the Bulli cops, to the people at the party Barnes had attended, to the witnesses at the crash site. I had to get details of Barnes Todd's business dealings from Michael Hickie and more from Felicia about his adventures in the art trade. Plenty to do to earn the money. It would take time and be hard on the nerves and tyres, but it was all comparatively straightforward compared to the tricky job of making contact with Kevin O'Fearna.

7

I hadn't drawn the blind and sunlight, bright and glaring, woke me early. I pulled the sheets and blanket up as I got out of them, which is about all the bedmaking I do these days. I collected the paper from the doorstep and noticed a real estate agent's leaflet I hadn't seen last night. "Ready to sell?" it asked. I looked up and could see the sky through a line of small holes in the rusty guttering above the porch. *Well, are you ready?* I thought.

I had some coffee and toast, read the paper, and took a walk around the streets and back lanes in the hope of seeing the cat. If I found the cat, I told myself, it meant I should stay in Glebe. I'd treat it better, feed it most days. I'd let it sleep on the couch. I wouldn't let the milk get sour. I'd make my bed. People were hosing their gardens, sitting on their balconies, hanging out their washing. Gaps were opening up along the sides of the streets as the workers took their cars away. I wandered down Wigram Road, where the cars are parked half on the footpath. Very illegal but very necessary in such a busy narrow street, and the cops seem to have accepted the practice.

I didn't find the cat.

By the time Felicia rang I was impatient to start work, and the O'Fear problem was nagging at me. "Hardy."

"You sound snappish," she said.

"Sorry. Where are you?"

"In a phone box close to home. I must say I quite like all this intrigue. No sign of the car you described last night, by the way."

"Good. I suppose you've got a few cameras?"

"Yes. Why?"

"Might be an idea if you sling one around your neck when you go out. It's a nervy feeling, following someone who's got a camera."

She laughed. "I can't go around with a bloody camera all the time. Mind you, I haven't taken any pictures for a while. It's a great day. Might be a good idea."

"What've you got planned for today?"

"Not much." The laughter went out of her voice.

"I suggest you ring Michael Hickie and talk a bit of business with him. Can you tell me anything about the party Barnes was at?"

"Yes. It was at a gallery in Paddington. Barnes was considering it for his exhibition. I've been to a million gallery parties. I couldn't face another one. Also I was afraid he'd get violent, and that was the one part of Barnes' personality I had trouble with. I went to the coast."

I got the name of the host and the address from her. I imagined her standing in the phone box or outside a shop. I wanted to see that brown hair in the sunlight. I wanted to see *her*. "I think you should go to this studio of yours tonight. Say before dinner. Leave your car and leave the house looking normal. Leave a light on, or the TV or something."

"Why?"

"I'll tell you tonight when I see you. Will you do it?"

Her characteristic pause again. Then she said, "Yes. All right."

"What's the address?"

"Flat two, 505 Chalmers Street, Redfern. It's opposite the park. There's no phone."

"I'll be there as soon as I can make it. Should I bring anything? Food, or . . . ?"

"No, it's well stocked. Just a minute."

"What? What's wrong?"

"Nothing. I'm just wondering why I'm letting you order me around like this."

I drew a deep breath. "I'm sorry. I didn't mean it to sound like that. There might be nothing happening or a simple explanation. I just think it's wise to take a few precautions."

"You're talking about the break-in and you being followed?"

"Yeah. And O'Fear's name coming up."

Another pause. Then her deep, breathy voice again. "All right. I'll play along for a while at least. See you at the studio tonight."

I shaved, carefully and closely. I had already shampooed my hair. I found a clean shirt and some cotton pants still wrapped in dry cleaner's plastic. Most of the wrinkles had dropped out of my jacket overnight. I'd pass muster in Paddington and Coogee. I might even get by in Redfern.

I suppose I started at the Paddington end of things because I thought it would be the easiest. Talk to a few arty types, confirm that Barnes hadn't been drunk at the party, and get a sceptical opinion on his chances of making millions as an artist. Bad practice to prejudge the outcome of an enquiry, but I've never known an enquirer who doesn't do it.

The Toby Cornwall Gallery was in Gipps Street. The street

bends sharply and the building that housed the gallery was built right on the dogleg, which gave it an odd, ramshackle shape. There was nothing shabby about it, though: outside it was all polished brass and heritage green paint; inside the walls and carpet were the same shade of just off-white. A soft light flooded down from a huge, tinted skylight. There were paintings on the walls and several more were hanging down into the open space, suspended on wires attached to the ceiling. Some sculptures sat on pedestals and there were things in glass cases I couldn't identify.

A few people were moving quietly around, looking at the exhibits and murmuring their appreciation. It looked like a good place to spend a lot of money, not much of a spot for a party. Felicia had told me that the director of the gallery was one Leon Willowsmith, who had eased out Toby Cornwall some time back. According to her, Willowsmith was a workaholic, never away from his shop. *Has to have an office somewhere,* I thought. *Can't do business out here. What if he spilled ink on the carpet?* I walked purposefully forward, ignoring the art, except when I had to swerve to avoid one of the hanging pictures. At the end of the room was a desk set beside a passageway. The expensive carpet stopped here and some darker, practical floor covering began. The business end, spill all the ink you like. A young, darkhaired woman sat at the desk thumbing through a glossy catalogue.

"Excuse me."

"Yes?" She looked up reluctantly; the catalogue was about antique jewellery.

"I'd like to see Mr. Willowsmith, please." I gave her a card.

She fumbled and dropped the card onto the catalogue. It didn't look much on top of a gold bracelet with a diamond clasp. "I don't know . . ."

"Tell him I'm working for Mrs. Barnes Todd."

She took the card, got up, and went down the passageway.

Her stiff, full skirt swished and she didn't hear me moving right behind her. She knocked on a door and opened it.

"Mr. Willowsmith, there's a private detective working for Felicia Todd. His name's . . ."

I pushed the door further open, took the card from her hand, and went past her. "Thank you," I said.

She grabbed my arm. "Hey!"

"Cliff Hardy, Mr. Willowsmith. Could you tell her to let me go? She might hurt me."

The man behind the desk had a pink, clean-shaven face and a pink, clean-shaven skull. He had massive shoulders inside a cream silk shirt. He smiled and something glinted on one of his large, white front teeth. "Mr. Hardy," he said. "Come in. I've been expecting you. It's all right, Judith. You can go."

Judith withdrew crossly and I walked towards the desk. Willowsmith held out his hand and I gave him the card.

"Excellent," he said. His voice was a soft purr. "Do sit down. A fine entrance—have you ever done any acting?"

I shook my head and sat in an uncomfortable chair made of canvas and tubular steel. The office was sparsely furnished with not an art object in sight. Willowsmith's desk held the usual clutter of the man who either was busy or wanted to look that way. He was taking all the points so far, which wasn't the way I'd intended things to go.

His remark had put me off balance. "What d'you mean, you were expecting me?"

He waved his right hand; the white, pudgy fingers carried at least three rings, maybe more. "You, or somebody like you. I knew Felicia would need some help. How can I be of assistance?"

I looked at him, trying to tell whether or not he was lying. It was impossible to say. His pale blue eyes were very steady and his thin mouth was firm—not that that means anything. He looked like a man who hires people to do things for him. Maybe watch houses and follow cars, but only for a very good reason. "I'm investigating Barnes Todd's death," I said. "I understand he attended a function here shortly before he died."

"Excuse me. Is this an insurance matter?"

"No."

"Then I don't understand."

There was something hypnotic about him. I found myself telling him briefly what my business was. He nodded as if he was used to people playing straight with him. "I could give you a list of the people who were here, with perhaps a few omissions. I think a couple of my guests were officially elsewhere in other company, if you follow me."

My turn to nod.

"Barnes certainly wasn't drunk. I doubt that he'd had more than one drink, two at most. He left quite late, but only because the argument took up a lot of time."

"Argument?"

"Oh, yes. I wanted to exhibit him. I'd sold some of his things privately. I thought I had the right. He objected to that. He became very angry."

"With you?"

"Yes, and with several other people in the business who tried to put their oars in. He called us the usual things—leeches, bloodsuckers and so on."

"You're being frank, Mr. Willowsmith."

He shrugged those big shoulders and smiled again. The glint came from a small diamond embedded in the tooth. "I have no choice. I want to exhibit him. I'm desperately anxious to do it. I assume you'll make a report on me to Felicia. I want it to be favourable. Would you like some coffee or something?"

"No thanks." I was finding his plausibility and frankness enough to cope with, without his hospitality. "You think Todd had a future as an artist?"

"Limitless—properly exhibited, properly handled and marketed."

"Have you seen a lot of his work?"

"No, have you?" The first note of an emotion not totally under control was struck then. His tone was sharp. He touched his smooth chin with his left hand, also heavy with rings.

I smiled non-committally. "What would a sizable collection of his work be worth?"

His eyes seemed to glitter like the diamond tooth, but that might have been just my imagination. "As I say, it would depend on who was handling it."

"Say you were handling it."

"Millions, over a period of time."

"Your competitors feel the same?"

"I have no competitors in this matter. Felicia should talk to me, no one else. I hope you can make that clear to her."

He moved slightly in his chair as he spoke. The purr was back in his voice and I thought I was beginning to read him. If I made the right noise I was sure he would offer me an inducement. It would have been a terribly wrong move for me. I took out my notebook and got the names of the other art dealers who had taken part in the heated conversation. He told me that Todd had left the party, which had been held in what he called an entertainment area further down the passage, at about 2 A.M. He had seemed very upset.

"Over the argument?" I asked.

The window behind Willowsmith was full of a view of the trees growing in some Paddington backyard. A stiff breeze had got up, and the trees were swaying. I wanted to be out in the wind; something about Willowsmith made me crave fresh air. He cleared his throat. "Possibly that, possibly something else. I'd have to say that he seemed upset when he arrived."

"Did you tell all this to the police?"

"Of course not."

"Why?"

"They didn't ask. I gave them some names and times. As I say, I've been frank with you, because . . ."

"You're desperate to get your hands on Barnes Todd's paintings."

"I wouldn't put it quite like that."

"Did you hear about the break-in at Barnes' house?"

"No. The paintings?"

"Nothing lost." His surprise and relief seemed genuine, but then, maybe Mr. Willowsmith had done some acting. I thanked him for his time and left the room. I waited outside with my ear to the door but he didn't pound the desk or grab the telephone. Maybe he counted his rings or felt his diamond with his tongue. Nasty sights, both. I walked out past Judith, who was looking at her catalogue again.

"Sorry I barged in like that," I said. "I was putting on my tough act."

She smiled warily. "That's okay. I bet it didn't worry him."

"You're right. Tell me, did you know Barnes Todd?"

"Mm, lovely man. I like his wife, too."

"Were you at the party?"

"Yes. I was serving drinks and things."

"Willowsmith tells me there was an argument. Did you see it?"

"Couldn't miss it. It was terrible. They were circling Mr. Todd like sharks."

I thanked her and left the gallery. So much for the softies of the art world. So much for starting at the easy end.

8

One of the many things you can do in Paddington is eat well. Lately I'd tended to eat when I was hungry, which wasn't necessarily at any particular hour or even three times a day. I bought a perfect apple and walked along Oxford Street eating it, looking at the fast-moving young and the slow-moving old and feeling somewhere in the middle. The shops seemed to be full of things that were more than a hundred years old or that had only been invented a week ago. I was on a promise to myself not to drink before six at least three times a week. Yesterday I'd buckled under at 10 A.M., today I was made of sterner stuff. I bought a takeaway coffee and put it in the slot under the orange phone where the directory was supposed to go.

Michael Hickie answered his own phone.

"You haven't had to let Jenny go, have you?" I said.

"Who's that?"

"Hardy. I was joking."

I could hear the relief in his voice over the traffic noise. "No, no. Her lunch break. Look, I want to thank you for talking to Felicia. She called me this morning and she was very reasonable about everything. She's given me the go-ahead to conclude a few pressing shipping and storage contracts, and we're going to have a meeting about the business as a whole. She's okaying your fee, by the way."

"Good. You sound a bit strained."

"One of these contracts of Barnes' is a bitch. I thought you might be someone from the opposition having a go at me."

"That rugged?"

"Packing and storing and development? You bet they're rugged. And Barnes was a pretty vigorous operator."

"That's what I'm ringing about. Is there anyone out at the Botany address who could tell me something about the business? I mean about competitors, dirty tricks, hands-on stuff?"

"There is. I was talking to him an hour ago after I spoke to Felicia. Bob Mulholland. He's your man, but he'll be busy now things are moving again."

"Could you give him a ring and tell him I'm coming over? I want to get cracking."

Hickie said he would. I rang off and drank the cool coffee. Paddington had a self-conscious, self-indulgent look. It was mark-up land, commission country, franchise-ville. I went to the Autobank, drew out a few judicious dollars for petrol and possible palm-greasing, got in the car and headed for Botany.

Barnes Enterprises was located off Botany Road, away from the water, a kilometre or so from the Caltex terminal. From a rise I could see the refinery structures in the distance—tall, spidery towers like something out of *The War of the Worlds.* Factories and houses jostled together in the streets. Some of the houses were solid and well maintained, but many looked apologetic about their existence. Their peeling paint and rusty metal said they were sorry to be there. I parked among trucks and utes and vans. Sydney these days seems to be filling up with leisure vehicles; VWs with their roofs cut off, four-wheel drives and convertibles, but here were only working wheels. A plane roared off the runway to the west, and the car shook as it passed over, gaining height. It left a dirty smudge in the clear blue sky and the noise stayed in my ears long after the plane became a speck.

I got out and almost had to fight for breath. I had a .45 automatic under the dashboard, a camera and miniature tape recorder among my professional equipment—what I really needed was a respirator. The dust in the air was clinging to the oily sludge and the slight breeze was stirring it all around like a chemical soup. And it was hot. Sweat broke out on my face; I wiped it off with my hand, which then felt greasy. I left my jacket in the car and walked between two prime movers and across a rutted piece of road to a wide double gate, standing open, in a high cyclone fence. It took massive posts and hinges to hold the gates, one of which had a metal plate attached to it, on which BARNES ENTERPRISES was written in fading red paint. Rust had pitted the metal and flaked off the paint so that the words were hard to read. The fence enclosed a couple of acres of cement, dirt, and scruffy grass. Along one perimeter was a large shed with a serrated roof; nearby were a couple of structures like aircraft hangars as well as smaller sheds and prefabs, all old. But one brick and glass structure was post-World War II. A few vehicles were in evidence—cars, vans, a loaded semi-trailer. There were a couple of sea cargo containers and several high stacks of wooden crates.

I had to jump aside to avoid a truck that raced past me through the gates. The driver jammed on the brakes and the truck threw up water and mud as it skidded through some puddles and stopped near the brick building. Three men wearing grey overalls jumped from the truck. One threw a brick through the window of a van, another began splashing something liquid from a can over the loaded semi-trailer. The first man went to work on truck tyres with a knife and the third ran a cable from the back of the truck towards a stack of crates.

I shouted and ran towards them. Two people came from the building, a man and a woman. The man threw himself at the one with the can and the woman ran in the direction of the nearest shed. When I got there, the man from the building had flattened the petrol splasher, but one of the others had king-hit him from behind. He sagged to his knees and his attacker got set to hit him again. He pulled the punch when he saw me and reached into his back pocket. I ducked under his swing and hit him very low with a wild right. The breath rushed from him and I heard metal hit the cement. I kicked him between the legs and he went down. The man with the knife was moving towards me, but I had the feeling he was happier slashing tyres. I grabbed the Stillson wrench the guy I'd put down had dropped and let him come. He stopped and the other two struggled up.

The woman had enlisted two men from the sheds. They were running towards us.

"Fuckin' hell," one of the attackers said. "I'm off!"

He ran for the truck and the other two went with him. I moved to follow them but the guy who had thrown the best punch of the fight was on his feet now. "Let the buggers go," he said.

They were twenty feet away and in the truck. They had left the motor running. *Stop them and we're talking to the police*, I thought. I threw the Stillson and it shattered the passenger side window as the truck roared off, spraying mud, the cable whipping along behind it.

The reinforcements reached us and one of the men sniffed loudly. "Shit, that's petrol."

"Are you all right, Bob?" the woman said.

"Yes, I'm all right." He turned to me. "I have to thank you, mate. You were bloody useful." He looked to be about fifty or a bit older, with the crinkly hair, dark skin, and wide nose of the

Aboriginal. He had boxing scars around his eyes and when I shook his hand I felt the lumpy knuckles of the ex-fighter. "Who are you, brother?"

"Cliff Hardy. If you're Bob Mulholland, I was coming to see you."

"That's me. Yeah, Mike Hickie told me. Excuse me a minute. Geoff, will you do something about the petrol? You'll need a hose and some sand. Col, can you take a look at the tyres?"

The men nodded. Col was the sniffer. He sniffed again. "Great throw with the Stillson, mate."

"Lucky," I said.

Mulholland brushed dirt from the knees of his grey pants. He wore a white shirt, no tie. Grey hair sprouted at the neck. "All in a day's work. This is Mrs. Carboni, Mr. Hardy."

"Anna," she said.

"Cliff," I said.

Mulholland mimed a short left jab and the solid right he had thrown a few minutes before. "Let's go inside. I could do with a cuppa tea."

We went up a short flight of concrete steps into the brick building which turned out to be the office. There was no air conditioning or interior decoration; it was a large work space with three desks, two computers, filing cabinets and notice boards covered with bits of paper. A couple of big maps of Sydney and suburbs hung on one wall; on another was a large blackboard with times, dates, and numbers scrawled on it in chalk. Anna Carboni asked whether I would rather have tea or coffee. I plumped for coffee the way I do a hundred times out of a hundred.

Mulholland settled into a chair and put his feet on the desk quite close to a computer. He gestured for me to pull another chair across. The computer screen was full of figures.

"Mike said you wanted to know a bit about the business. What you've just seen isn't typical."

"I'd be surprised if it was. But you're not interested in calling the police?"

He shrugged. "I didn't see the number of their truck, did you?"

I tried to remember. "I don't think it had one."

"There you are. The cops couldn't help even if they wanted to, which is only even money. I blame myself. Things've been very quiet and I got slack. I should've kept a look out. Barnes would have roasted me for leaving those bloody gates open."

Anna came back from the sink and urn at the far end of the room with three mugs. She gave me mine, Mulholland his, and sat at one of the desks. She tapped computer keys.

"Thanks, Anna, you make a great cuppa." Mulholland said.

She smiled. "For a wog."

"You can't help being a New Australian." He grinned at me, which puckered the smooth scar tissue and made slits of his eyes. "Neither can you."

"Right," I said. Through the window I could see Geoff, Col, and another man working in the yard. The big gates were closed. "How much did Michael Hickie tell you?"

Mulholland sipped his black tea. "About you? Nothing. Just said to help you any way I can."

"Barnes thought someone might try to kill him," I said. Anna Carboni's head jerked aside, but she kept her eyes on the screen in front of her. "What do you think of that?" I was addressing both of them, but Mulholland answered.

"I warned him a coupla times that he was taking too many bloody risks, cutting corners, going at it too fast. But . . . did you know him?"

"Yes."

"Well, he did what you'd expect. Tightened the security around here and other places and made sure the accident insurances were paid up, but he didn't do a bloody thing about his personal safety. What brings you into it?"

I told him while he finished his tea.

"Drink your coffee before it gets cold." His voice, gruff and harsh, as it is with most older Aborigines, sounded almost hostile. "I wish he'd told me he felt that way. Maybe I coulda helped him. Given it a bloody good go, anyhow."

I drank the coffee. Anna Carboni had stopped working; she gazed across the top of the computer monitor. "He was a strong man," she said. "The best I ever worked for."

Mulholland nodded. I told them that Felicia Todd was having discussions with Hickie about the future of the business. They listened and seemed comforted. Anna was in her forties—these were not good times for people at their stage of life to be thrown out of work. I explained that I wanted a rundown on the business: number of employees and details about them, long-term contracts, new jobs, sub-contracting, competition.

"Do you know who your visitors today were, for instance?"

"I'd guess they were from Riley's," Mulholland said. "Just a dumb stunt to keep us on the ropes."

"Who's Riley?"

"Big operator. One of the biggest, before Barnes came along and undercut him and provided a better service right across the board. Riley had a big slice of trucking, storage, and house removal, all dovetailed but bloody expensive and ratshit managed."

"What's house removal?"

"It's all the go. People want old houses off their land to build new things, other people want houses already built. We cut 'em in half and move 'em on low loaders. Supply and demand."

"Sounds tricky."

"It is, but there's money in it. Riley had councillors in his pocket all over the state. Coppers too. Big kickbacks all round. You need council approval, see? And police co-operation on the roads. Barnes went to the local MPs and the straight councillors and got the game cleaned up. Riley didn't like it."

"This seems like a pretty crude operation for a big wheel."

"Riley's like that. We've lost a lot of business since Barnes died. I've had to put people off. Riley's picked up our crumbs, but I think he wants to wipe us out altogether."

"So this wasn't the first trouble here?"

Mulholland firmed his jaw muscles and shook his head in the way fighters do to loosen up. "First in daylight. There were a couple of pathetic goes at the office a while back. A shot at burning down a shed. Nothing we couldn't handle."

"What sort of money's involved?" I said.

"If you mean what's up for grabs between Barnes Enterprises and some of the other big operators, it's fairly complicated," Anna said. She touched the computer screen. "I could prepare a breakdown for you, but it'll take me a few days. Do you happen to know how Mrs. Todd is?"

"She's fine," I said. "Well . . . picking up."

Mulholland seemed to be having trouble controlling a hostile spasm. "How come she's taking an interest all of a sudden? That your doing?"

I shrugged. "I might have helped a bit."

The scar-puckering grin again. "You're all right, Cliff. Anna, you want some overtime?"

She nodded eagerly. The working relationship between them seemed to be excellent, and it is axiomatic that a good boss gets and keeps good workers. All the signs were that here at least Barnes Todd was surrounded by loyalty and efficiency.

"Get the stuff he needs together." He took his feet from the desk. "Fancy a walk? I'll show you over the place."

For the next hour we walked from shed to shed, looked over the storage and maintenance areas, loading and unloading docks. We talked in bursts, frequently interrupted by the noise of the planes.

"Pretty big show," I said.

"Was getting bigger." He rubbed the back of his neck where he had taken the hard rabbit punch.

"Sore head?"

"Nah. Just a tap. Had 'em harder than that, as you can probably tell."

"Where did you fight?"

"Everywhere. Fought for the state welter title. Lost on points. But I won a few."

I pointed to three identical gunmetal blue Ford Lasers parked in the shadow of a container. "What're they for? Staff cars?"

Mulholland laughed. "They went out with the FBT tax. No, Barnes was pretty pissed off with the security service we were using. He was playing around with the idea of setting up his own."

We were back at the office. Anna was about to start work on compiling data for me. She flourished a floppy disk. "How do you want it, Cliff? On disk, tape, paper, what?"

"I want it secure," I said. "Very, very secure."

9

"I'm for a beer," Bob Mulholland said. "Cliff?"

It was after five o'clock. He packed some papers into a Gladstone bag, took a light jacket off a peg and had a few words with Anna about locking up her computer disks and the security of the buildings and yards.

"We've got alarms all around," he told me as we walked towards the front gate. "Two night watchmen and a couple of dogs. It's pretty good."

We went through the gate. "No car?" I said.

"Nah, I live in Mascot. Walk to work. Keeps the fat down."

I couldn't see much fat and he walked briskly, but I had the feeling that it had been a long day for him and maybe the rabbit punch had hurt him more than he let on. He accepted the offer of a lift gratefully. He settled into the seat and stretched his legs. The Gladstone bag sat between his feet.

"Good car?"

I started the engine, which ran smoothly and softly.

"Sounds all right. Had it long?"

"Not long. I traded its older brother in on it. I like Falcons, don't ask me why."

He laughed. "I like Holdens. Don't know why either. Let's go to the Beauchamp. On Botany Road."

We didn't speak on the short drive. Mulholland stared straight in front of him. He sighed once, deeply. I realised that he was very tired indeed.

The pub was old and on a corner, the way a pub should be. It also boasted Sky Channel TV, which I'm not so sure about. After the chemical gunge outside, the air, filled with the aromas of beer, smoke, and sweat, seemed almost fresh. We went into the public bar and Mulholland settled his bag between his legs, as workmen have done for centuries. "I owe you one. That Stillson would've made a mess of me. What'll it be?"

We both had middies of old and sank them quickly, without talking. Mulholland knew the barman and a few of the other drinkers. They acknowledged him respectfully. I'd seen ex-boxers get that kind of reception before, but usually those who kept on using their fists. Mulholland's respect seemed to carry a tinge of affection as well.

"My buy." I got the next round. The beer tasted good and I was happy to be there drinking it. But I knew he hadn't invited me along just for the company.

When we were halfway through the second round Mulholland said, "Let's go and sit down. I'm bushed."

We sat at a table with a wet surface and full ashtray but as far as possible from the men gathered rowdily around the giant TV screen. The barman hurried over and wiped away the slops. He also removed the ashtray.

"You've got clout in here," I said.

Mulholland sipped his beer. "Worked around here most of my life. Ever since I got down from the bush. I've done everything —truckie, storeman, maintenance at Caltex, the lot."

"How long have you worked for Barnes?"

"Fifteen years, no, eighteen. From the beginning." He snorted. "He made me go to night school, would you believe it? I was thirty-five, a boong from the bush, bloody near illiterate. Hardly a thought in m' head."

"How did you meet him, Bob?"

"Korea. He was my C.O."

"I thought they only took veterans from the war in Korea."

"No, I was with the occupation mob in Japan. They took a few of us."

"You must've been young."

He grinned. "Joined in forty-nine when I was sixteen. Used the birth certificate of an uncle of mine who was a few years older. No one knew. That "all boongs look alike" stuff was operating, you know."

I realised that I didn't know anything about Barnes Todd's war record except what he'd told me. That was all anecdotal, throwaway stuff. Knowledge is the name of my game. "What sort of an officer was he?"

"The best. Were you in the service, Cliff?"

"Malaya."

"I thought that was before Korea."

"It started before, but it went on a lot later. I was in at the very end. Tell me about Barnes."

"Not that much to tell. We were in the Third Battalion, A Company. Saw a hell of a lot of action—up to Manchuria and down to Seoul and back to the parallel."

"Frostbite Ridge?"

"My oath. Barnes looked after us. Bloody brilliant soldier. Whole thing was a waste of time, of course, but I didn't know that then."

He finished his drink so abruptly that I thought he was about to leave, but he took out five dollars. "Three's my limit," he said. "Mind getting 'em? Get a glass of water too, would you?"

There was a soccer match on the TV and the singlet-, overall- and T-shirt-wearing men were shouting and swearing as they drank and watched. The carpet in front of the TV set was worn through to the underlay. The walls and ceiling were stained from the cigarette fug that enveloped the watchers. When I got back with the drinks, he had two pills in the pink palm of his hand. He flicked them into his mouth and swallowed them with the water. "Bit of heart trouble. Nothing serious. Cheers."

We drank some more beer and he told me about his few years as a boxer after he had come back from Korea. Then it had been dead-end jobs for a long time until by chance he had met up with Barnes Todd, who was just getting started in his trucking business.

He did a good imitation of Barnes' bluff manner and voice. "First, you'll need an education, corporal."

"That's him," I said.

"He was as good at business as he had been at soldiering," Bob said. "Bloody tough, but fair. He looked after you."

"How d'you mean?"

"Started up a super scheme as soon as he could afford it. Pretty democratic about the big decisions, asked everyone's opinion, at least. There's a bit of profit-sharing among the workers. I mean, it's not bloody utopia or anything, but a hell of a lot better than the average."

"Was he always on the up and up?"

"Pretty much, as far as I know. Early on we did a few things that wouldn't stand up to too much examination. Cleaned out a few warehouses for people. Debatable, I'd call it. Nothing really bent. D'you want details? It was a long time ago and pretty small beer."

I shook my head. "Did you know he was a painter? A good one, they say."

"No, but it doesn't surprise me."

The noise in the pub had gone up as the workers had come in

after knocking off; there was no one close and little danger of being overheard, but Bob leaned closer to me. "Was he murdered?"

"I don't know. What d'you reckon? I was hoping the business records might give me a clue."

"They might."

"But you don't think so. Come on, Bob. Something's on your mind. I need all the help I can get."

"It's probably nothing," Mulholland muttered. "But I can't get it out of m' head. It happened at Wonsan, on the retreat. We pulled back with the Yanks, except that they were running and we were fighting."

"I've heard about it," I said.

"Yeah, no sense in going over it again. Most of 'em were conscripts so it wasn't their fault. Throw in a few bad officers and you've got all the makings of a balls-up. You never saw anything like the mess at Wonsan—the port was choked with boats trying to get away, the roads were shot to shit. What with the smoke and the rain, it was hard to tell who was who and what was what." An old-soldier look came over his face. The look holds two things in balance; thank God I'm out of it, and Christ, what a time it was!

He sipped some beer and went on, "Our platoon was down to five men and were buggered. We'd been on the move without sleep for days, almost no food and a couple of us with wounds. Barnes was holding us together, but only just."

His dark face took on a fixed, strained look as if the act of memory was ageing him. I didn't say anything.

"The Yanks had had to abandon most of their armour, most of their transport and supplies. They were demoralised. Weather was too bad for the planes and a lot of the Yanks were still recovering from their first sight of the Chinese up close. Scary's not the word for those blokes."

"I know." I had my own memories of the fanatical little Chinese fighters. In Malaya we hadn't had endless waves of them like in Korea, but ten at a time were quite enough.

"There was this American captain trying to get clear in a jeep. He shot a couple of civilians, including a woman and a kid, who got in his way. He ran over two wounded men. Barnes jumped onto the jeep and put his Webley up the captain's nose. He made him stop to pick people up, Koreans mostly. We sort of escorted the jeep to where the medics were working and Barnes made a report on the captain."

"You saw all this?"

"Not exactly. I'd copped one in the head. Nothing much, bit of metal I reckon. But it blinded me temporarily and buggered me up a bit. Barnes was hauling me along like a side of meat. I heard some of the shots and shouting. Barnes told me about it all later."

"What sort of a report did he make? Who to?"

"I'm not sure. It was all a bloody mess. The mortars were dropping around us and the Yanks were firing everything they had in all directions at once. But I heard the captain just before we moved on. He said, "I'll kill you, you bastard, if it's the last thing I do." It was as if everything stopped moving and all the noise stopped and I could hear every word. That's how I remember it although it wasn't like that, of course. I can still hear the captain's voice. I mean he was a mad dog to start with, and what Barnes did really hit him. He meant it."

"It's nearly forty years ago," I said.

"It's yesterday in my head. I know it's crazy, but when I heard this talk of Barnes being murdered, it's the first thing I thought of."

I said I'd be in touch to collect the results of Anna Carboni's work and to talk some more. We shook hands. He declined my offer of a lift home, saying he'd walk off the beer. As I watched him stride away, swinging his Gladstone bag, I realised that I knew nothing about his personal life. Did he have a wife, kids? He'd impressed me as an intelligent, truthful man, but what if I was wrong? What if he harboured a corrosive grudge against his WASP ex-C.O. and had waited thirty-plus years for an opportunity to settle the score?

I knew it was the beer on an empty stomach talking, and I took a walk to clear my head and give myself a chance of getting below .05. The planes kept taking off and touching down; it was just as well I was talking to myself because the human voice wouldn't have stood a chance above the racket. *Now you've got three suspects—someone in the art game, a business rival, and a U.S. Army captain. Good going. Throw in Mulholland and the widow and you're really in business. And what about suicide?* That reminded me I should talk to Todd's doctor. My business mainly consists of paying visits on people, some welcome, some not. And ten grand buys a lot of visits.

10

On the drive from Botany to Redfern, I tried to sift the facts and
impressions I'd acquired so far, but two things kept distracting
me—the prospect of seeing O'Fear in Long Bay and my urgent
need for a piss. It was no way to go calling on a lady.

On the drive through Mascot, Rosebery, and Alexandria,
there's nothing to inspire higher feelings. The residents of Alexandria are still waiting for their long-promised park on the old
brickworks and rubbish dump site. It was strange—there was a
state election campaign running and I hadn't heard a word about
speeding up work on the park. I amused myself by trying to work
out what that meant. I decided that it was a forecast of the
election result—the government thought it was going to lose so
there was no point in talking about the park and the opposition
didn't have to talk about it because it thought it was going to
win.

I had the piss and bought some white wine in a pub in Pitt
Street. This part of Redfern was very quiet, almost sedate. There

were designer denim shops and Thai restaurants. I paid more for the wine than I expected to, a sure sign that an area is on the rise. I drove around the park and adjacent streets, partly to familiarise myself with an area that seemed to have changed dramatically since the last time I'd been in it, and partly to see if K blank M 2s and 3s was around. I didn't see it.

Near the park and for a few streets around, a lot of the houses had been renovated. Big three-storeyed terraces and little single-fronted cottages had all had the treatment. Iron lace was back; the fibro and louvres had been knocked out of the balconies and vines grew out of tubs and tangled round where washing had once hung. Tons of cement had been prised up from front and back gardens and greenery was sprouting over the fences. Even the park had had a facelift; the big old trees looked healthy and there were wild thickets of new growth that contrasted well with the orderly layout of the paths, fountain, and war memorial.

The last of the useful light went as I parked in Chalmers Street a few doors from number 505. It was one of the two-storeyed jobs, all sandblasted brick, wrought iron, and clean tiles. It occurred to me that this was what the next owner would probably do to my house. I shrugged into my jacket, took a grip on the wine, and pushed open the gate.

My knock brought quick footsteps on the stairs and Felicia Todd opened the door. She was wearing white pants and a blue silk shirt knotted at the waist. She looked fresh and almost happy. I was suddenly aware of a strong wish to keep her that way.

"Well," she said. "You look like you've had a hard day."

I rubbed my hand across my bristly chin. "That bad?"

"I didn't say bad."

"I've just come from Mascot where the workers really work. I can tell you that you're pretty popular out there just now."

She smiled and patted the bottle under my arm. "What's that? Some plonk?"

"Yes. I thought . . ."

"Look, Cliff, herb omelette's about my limit. If you want to wine and dine, we'd better go out."

"I don't care. A sandwich'll do me."

"No, I'd like to get out." She stuck her head through the door and mimed a furtive look up and down the street. "Is it safe?"

"It's getting cool. You'll need a jacket."

She went quickly up the stairs. My nasty suspicious mind wondered whether she had contrived a way to keep me out. Distrust is an occupational hazard; Cyn said I must have distrusted my mother. Felicia came back wearing a grey denim jacket with the fashionable half-worn-out look. She felt in her pocket for the key and slammed the door hard. We stood on the pavement and faced west.

"Italian? Chinese? Thai? What?" she said.

"No Greek?"

"We can do Greek. D'you like Greek?"

"Yeah, I do, as a matter of fact."

"So do I. Greek it is."

We walked to a restaurant in Elizabeth Street. She told me she had filled in the day pretty much as she had expected, with walking and taking photographs. She was animated, apparently glad of my company. But then she'd had a boring day.

I was so hungry I wouldn't have cared what nationality the food was, but the flat bread, skewered lamb, and salad were good. Felicia knocked off a glass of wine quickly and then nursed a second for the rest of the meal. I gave her an outline of what I had done during the day. She looked concerned when I told her about the disturbance at Mascot.

"Was Bob hurt?" she said.

"No. They got more hurt than us."

"You sound like Barnes. Tell me about the place. I've only been out there once or twice, and very briefly."

"It's worth a visit," I said. "I'll take you next time." I told her about Anna Carboni and the work she was doing for me.

"It's funny," she said, when I finished talking to do some more chewing.

"What is?"

"You met the most hateful person Barnes knew, that's Willowsmith, and the nicest—Bob Mulholland. You must be getting some interesting impressions."

"Willowsmith struck me as dangerous."

"He is. I could tell you some stories."

We were picking at the remains of the salad by this time. I dipped a bit of bread in the dressing. "Bob Mulholland told me something interesting." I gave her the story about the U.S. captain.

"Barnes used to have nightmares about Korea. I came to hate the sound of the word. Could there be anything in that, d'you think?"

"It seems unlikely. Barnes never mentioned it? No strange Americans turned up recently?"

The waiter cruised up and we ordered coffee. I let him take away the wine bottle with more than an inch still in it. I hoped I was making a good impression. We sat quietly watching the other diners while we waited for the coffee. There was only one smoker and only two people were noticeably affected by alcohol. Times have changed in Redfern and everywhere else. I caught a snatch of conversation about the election: "Political parties are a conspiracy against the people. They're *both* in trouble." I was in agreement; maybe I'd have to revise my analysis of the Alexandria park issue.

Felicia sipped her coffee. "There *was* an American business type Barnes had some dealings with. It was last year. Constable or Sheriff or some name like that . . . I forget. Michael Hickie'd have the details."

I took out my notebook, wrote "Constable?/Sheriff?" and sighed.

"Is this getting you down already, Cliff? I thought you were Mr. Stick-at-it."

I laughed. She had that effect on me. "Sounds Yugoslav."

"And in fact you are . . . ?"

"English and Irish. What about you?"

"The same," she said.

The waiter had left the brass coffee pot on the table. I poured some more for both of us. "No, I'm not disheartened. I was just wondering where O'Fear fitted into all this."

"Ah, yes. O'Fear. Maybe he doesn't fit."

"I've got a feeling he does. There's no problem seeing him in the context of Barnes' business activities. I'd be willing to bet he's driven a truck at some stage, and I'm pretty sure he was in Korea."

She raised her eyebrows at the disliked word. "What about art and such?"

I had good reasons for not wanting to go to Long Bay but I must have sounded surly when I spoke. "I don't know. He was a folk singer and a Celtic revival nut. He might have done watercolours of Galway Bay for all I know."

"You're a strange man, Cliff Hardy," Felicia said. "You're half charm and half ill-temper. Just like . . ."

She didn't finish but I had a fair idea what name she had in mind. It was a moderately awkward moment. We finished our coffee. I paid the bill and we left. It was a nice, mild night, perfect for a stroll around the park or a quiet drink on the balcony in Chalmers Street or a number of other things. But we weren't going to do any of them. Barriers of guilt and repression were going up fast: the English and the Irish.

As we turned for home I asked her where the paintings and photographs were.

"Safe," she said.

"I hope they're not at Thirroul. That's . . ."

"The first place anyone would look. I know. What if I told you they're scattered around? Here and there?"

"That'd be smart."

She nodded and lengthened her stride to keep up with me. I hadn't realised that I'd increased my speed. "What's your next move?"

"I'll see O'Fear tomorrow. That reminds me, I should talk to Barnes' doctor."

"Why?"

"It's standard."

"What are you implying? He was in the peak of health."

Things were getting sticky. "Okay," I said. "If you say so. Now I'm going to Coogee."

"Why?"

"To see if that car's anywhere near your house."

She didn't say anything more as we walked at a slower pace. The park was across the road, dark but not threatening. The lights that marked the paths gleamed through the trees. The leaves were moving in the light breeze. We stopped outside number 505.

"How long d'you think I should stay here?" she said.

I shrugged. "Depends. A couple of nights."

"I'd like to go to the coast."

"I'll talk to you tomorrow. Might know something more by then."

She clinked her keys in her pocket and I thought she was leaving, but she put her arm half around me, reached up and kissed me on the cheek. "Be careful," she said.

I did the slow circuit of the streets around the park again with the same result. Then I headed for Coogee. It was a high-mileage day. One of the penalties of the job. The meat and bread had soaked up the wine and the strong coffee was doing its job. Metabolically I was in good shape; emotionally not so good. Something was happening between me and Felicia Todd and I had the uncomfortable feeling that neither of us was in control of it.

It was a magic night in Coogee. The waves were curling up and lying down quietly, hitting the beach like a soft drumbeat, and the sky was clear out over the sea. Above the land were light, high clouds, the kind that obscure the moon for a few minutes and then move on. No sign of the car in question. I parked a hundred metres from the Todd house and walked along the quiet street. You don't have to be in a car to watch a place. I've watched from roofs in my time, even from trees. The wild, scarcely tended front garden was ideal for watching. A couple of lights were on inside, but I expected that. I didn't expect the shadow that moved, low and fast, in the front room.

I didn't have a gun; I didn't have any weapon except my ill-humour. I pushed open the gate and began to move towards the house, keeping to the cover provided by the shrubs and bushes. I searched with one hand for something to throw or hit with, but found nothing. I reached the side of the big front porch, which was high above ground level. The set of steps leading directly up to the porch and front door was bathed in moonlight. I swore under my breath, slipped out of my jacket, and stuck my foot in the latticework under the porch. With a bit of a jump and grab I could pull myself up over the rail. I jumped and grabbed and pulled.

My shirt ripped, but that was the only sound I made. I tested the boards on the porch and found them solid. The front door was standing slightly open. I took two cautious steps towards it. A car horn honked twice loudly and I heard a squeal of tyres. I looked in the direction of the sounds and saw a car accelerate past the house and skid around the side street. I jumped forward, shoved the door open, and ran into the house. I was halfway down the passage when I heard glass breaking at the back. The dog next door howled. I dashed through to the kitchen. The glass door that led to the terrace was wide open with one of its panes smashed. Glass crunched under my feet as I looked out at the yard; the fence was low and the drop to the street wasn't much. You'd be unlucky to hurt yourself getting over it. No blood on the floor. A clean getaway.

The dog stopped howling and no lights came on in the house or the flats around. So much for neighbourliness. I went through the house, which had been thoroughly and messily searched. The alarm had been professionally short-circuited at one of the windows. I turned off the television set, which was showing a state government advertisement about how good things were and how they were going to get better. I cut the palm of my right hand cleaning up the glass and ran water on the cut. The water turned red as it flowed out of the sink. First blood to the other side—whoever they were.

The shirt was a write-off. I ripped the sleeve out and used it to tie up the cut, which was bleeding freely. I locked the back door and pulled the front door shut. Anyone watching would have seen a man with a bleeding hand, dirty pants, and a torn shirt rummaging in the shrubbery for his jacket. But I could probably have dug a grave or danced the carioca—no one was looking.

On the drive home to Glebe I tried to figure it out. I concluded that someone knew Felicia Todd wasn't at home. Did that mean they knew where she was now? Probably. I could imagine a watcher phoning through the message to the searcher that Mrs. Todd was going to be busy for the night. But the night had ended abruptly. Was she in danger? Probably not. These people seemed to avoid confrontation. Some comfort in that. Not much. The cut hand throbbed and the rough bandage made driving difficult. I made the turn into my street clumsily and rammed the gutter with my tyres when I stopped.

My house smelled of damp. At least it didn't smell of cat. I was in a foul mood. I cleaned the cut, put a dressing on it, and went to bed. I was almost asleep when the thought came. *Two honks probably meant trouble at the front, three meant the back.* Smarter than me. I shouldn't have looked at the street. As soon as I heard the noise, I should have gone straight in.

11

As it happened, I knew Kevin O'Fearna's solicitor slightly. Brian
Dolan was one of the old school of city lawyers, slightly tarnished
by long association with politicians but never mentioned in an
enquiry, never newsworthy. I phoned him and confirmed that
O'Fear was still on remand.

"When does his case come up?" I asked.

"The police are having trouble with the witnesses. What's
your interest, Mr. Hardy?"

Dolan was a man you instinctively lied to. "A non-legal matter. Just out of curiosity, what would his bail be?"

"It's ten thousand dollars, which is a bloody scandal."

I felt a sinking feeling in my stomach. "Wouldn't his mates be
able to put that up?"

"Kevin doesn't exactly have any mates just now."

O'Fear had once told me that only lawyers and priests called
him Kevin. I hoped I wouldn't be talking to any priests. I cut off
Dolan's next question, thanked him, and hung up. A call to

Long Bay got me a tedious wait on the line and then a 10:45 A.M. visiting slot. I told them I was working for Cy Sackville, which was a lie, but they're used to lies at Long Bay.

Visiting a prisoner is taking a punt. He can always change his mind and refuse to see you, which is his right. It's not a bad trick for a bored inmate to play on an outsider. Luckily, O'Fear wasn't much given to boredom. He was a regular gaolhouse lawyer by all accounts and, when he wasn't giving advice, he was probably gambling, or talking or singing. I turned off Anzac Parade, parked in a side street, and walked back. It was a sunny morning with a light breeze, but neither that nor the flower beds beside the long, grey concrete ramp to the barrier could make the place cheerful. The guy in the glasshouse checked me over and waved me through to the entrance. I filled in my slip, writing clumsily with the bandaged hand, gave it to one of the beefy Ulstermen who run the place, and sat down on the wooden bench next to the rubber tree plant and the other visitors.

Over the years I've visited a good many men in Long Bay. Those visits tend to blur into one mostly depressing memory. Much sharper is the recollection of the time I spent here on remand myself. The second case I handled as a private detective involved a runaway girl. I found the girl and I also found that her father had been committing incest with her since she was ten. I wasn't tactful or understanding. I put the father in hospital and the girl and the mother told the police that I had assaulted and robbed him. I was new at the game and out of my territory in Parramatta. I was wary of the cops, and my lawyer knew less law than I did. I was only at the Bay for ten days, but that was bad enough. In gaol you get more insults and abuse in a day than in ten years on the outside. Since then, they tell me, it's got worse. If the screws have become a bit more careful in dealing out abuse, the crims have got more reckless. In my time sex was mostly in the prisoners' heads; now it's on the floor and in the toilets and no pleases and thank yous.

When you visit a convicted prisoner you have to submit to a thorough search and deposit most of your belongings in a locker. Visitors to people on remand get a less rigorous going-over. Still, the guard prodded at my bandage and snarled back at me when I swore. He let me into the visiting room and told me to sit and wait.

"How long?" I said.

"Long as it takes," the guard said. From the look on his hard, pale face, the only thing that'd make him smile would be the sound of bone breaking.

I took a deep breath and sat in the chair facing the door. It was a small room with lino tiles on the floor and a dusty window set too high up to reach. The pale yellow light indicated reinforced glass. The table and two chairs were bolted to the floor. The ashtray was plastic and deeply scarred by crushed-out butts. I recalled that I crushed out a few hundred in my ten days. Prison air has a nasty smell; it feels bad for your lungs. Maybe that's why everyone smokes so much—the smoke can't be worse for you than the air.

The door opened and O'Fear came in. He stopped for dramatic effect and to make a pretence of tipping the guard. He stood about five foot eight and had a wrestler's build—huge shoulders and a barrel chest. His waistline expanded and contracted according to his circumstances. Just now, he was trim.

"Cliff, boy," he bellowed. "Long time no seizure." He roared with laughter at his own joke and rushed across towards me. I stood and he put a bear hug on me. It was eleven o'clock in the morning and he was in prison, but he still smelled of whisky.

"Hello, O'Fear. How are they keeping you?"

He gave my joke a smaller laugh and reached for my hand. I pulled it away and showed him the dressing.

"What've you been doing to yourself, Cliff?"

"Just a scratch."

"It'll play hell with your sex life." He laughed again and took the other chair. He looked the picture of well-being; his red hair was streaked with grey but thick; his skin was lightly tanned and clear, and his eyes and teeth shone. He looked as if he'd been spending time at a flash health farm. "There's no one I'd rather see, Cliff, 'cept me dear mother, and she passed away ten year ago, God rest her soul."

"Cut it out, O'Fear," I said. "Could we have a small ban on the phoney Irish stuff?"

"You're in a bad mood, I see. How Irish are yez again? I forget."

"Two grandmothers. They gave their husbands hell."

"Ah yes, they would. Irishwomen are the devil—they either love God or themselves and no man at all." He examined his hands, which were small and clean. It was a long time since O'Fear had pushed a wheelbarrow. When he spoke again, it was in ordinary, inner-Sydney Australian. "What can I do for you?"

"How d'you like it here?"

"It's a shit hole. The ignorance in here is shocking."

"What're your chances?"

"It's hard to say. It's a conspiracy, of course. That's what the police are best at. You haven't come here to discuss my case, Hardy, or to have me sing you a song. What's on your mind?"

"Barnes Todd."

"Ah. Poor man."

I watched his reaction very closely, but O'Fear was an experienced performer and I couldn't read anything in his clear blue eyes or the set of his curling Irish mouth. "I'm enquiring into his death."

"On whose behalf? The widow's?"

I nodded. This was a tricky course to steer. I wanted O'Fear to do the talking, to learn as much as I could from him before having to offer him anything in return. But O'Fear knew when to talk and when to shut up. He said nothing.

"I understand you might have some information for me."

He let a bit of the Irish lilt back into his voice. "Now, how would you be reachin' an understandin' like that?"

"I thought we were going to do without the blarney?"

"Okay." That was the first sign I had, that quick compliance. He wanted out. I had to follow up the advantage.

"How well did you know Todd?"

"If I tell you that, will you tell me how my name came up?"

The points on that exchange would probably go to him, but I didn't have much choice. "Yes."

"I knew Barnes a long time. More than thirty years. I met him in Korea and I worked for him at various times—borrowed money, this and that."

"Ever do anything dodgy?"

"Who? Me?"

"I'm told there was a time when he sailed a bit close to the wind. Moved things that perhaps should've stayed where they were."

He grinned the way a man with good teeth can. "I neither confirm nor deny, and I don't have any details."

"D'you know anything about his painting?"

He held up his hand. "You've had your whack, Cliff. Give a little."

I told him that his name was on Barnes Todd's lips when he died. O'Fear was no hypocrite; he took the information as an interesting fact, not an occasion for sentiment. He nodded but said nothing.

"Do you know what that might mean?" I said.

"You think he was murdered, do you?"

"Why d'you say that?"

"I'm guessing." He sat back in his chair and showed the million-dollar teeth in his ten-dollar Irish mug. "I think I can help you," he said.

My cut hand was throbbing. I rubbed it lightly and looked up at the dirty window. "If?"

"If you get me out of here."

"I suppose I could have a word with Dolan."

"Bugger Dolan. Irish prick. Who's your lawyer?"

"Cy Sackville, as you very well know."

"What sort of money d'you make these days, Cliff boy?" He reached over and took the lapel of my jacket between his thumb and forefinger. "You never put it on your back, but you look prosperous enough." He ducked his head under the table. "And you're wearing *shoes!*"

I sighed. "I'm on a flat ten thousand fee for this job."

His toothy grin became a broad smile. It was the sort of smile he used to flash in the smoky folk clubs before he broke into "The shoals of herring." He held out his left hand for me to shake. "There you are, now. Sure it must be part of a grand plan."

We shook, left-handedly, which is probably bad luck or something. Anyone watching might have thought we were members of a secret society. Perhaps we were—the friends of Barnes Todd.

12

"Why don't you get Sackville to do it?" Michael Hickie said.

I juggled the coffee Jenny had brought me on my knee. "It's good experience for you, Mike. You don't want to become a grey corporate lawyer, do you? All balance sheets and no balls? This is where the action is—posting bail, 'on his own recognisances' and all that."

"What happened to your hand?"

"I cut it cleaning up the glass the burglar broke in Felicia Todd's kitchen. See what I mean? That's the workface." I was in a good mood and I knew why. The prospect of visiting Long Bay had been depressing me and I felt the load float away after I'd done the job and left. Also, I was glad to be putting one over on O'Fear. He thought he was getting Sackville and he was getting Hickie instead. Tough luck. You had to keep your guard up with O'Fear; he tended to favour the steamroller approach.

Hickie grinned. "I could feel patronised, but I don't. I'll get onto it straight away. Shouldn't take more than a day or two."

He squinted down at the notes he had taken from me about O'Fear. "You said there was something else?"

"Two things. First, Mrs. Carboni is putting together a profile of Barnes' business activities. I assume that's the operational end. Would you know about the contracts, correspondence, and such?"

He nodded. "You'd get most of it from Anna. Barnes believed in open government. The people who worked for him could see the paper on the deals if they wanted to. I've got a few things, strictly legal, that wouldn't be at Mascot. If Felicia okayed it, you could see them. What did you think of Bob Mulholland?"

"Great bloke." I told him about the incident at Mascot.

"Stanley Riley's a madman, according to Barnes," he said. "Good thing you were there."

"Everything'll be tighter now that things are running again. How busy will they be?"

"Very. Quite a few jobs on hold to clear. I can go ahead with some leasing of space for storage and make applications for licences to ship some stuff."

"What?"

"Chemicals. You need special trucks, special licences. It was all going through when Barnes died."

"Why was he getting into that?"

Hickie shrugged. "He said it had to be done, so it might as well be done right. The money's good." He saw me looking dubious and he went on, "I should tell you that he was moving towards transporting radioactive waste."

I groaned. "Jesus, this gets worse and worse. The greenies might've taken him out."

Hickie put on what I took to be his pragmatic face. "You said there were two things you wanted."

"Yeah. I'm interested in a Yank Barnes had some dealings with last year. Felicia knew about him, but she didn't know his name. What can you tell me?"

The coffee was cold; I put my mug on the desk, but Hickie drained his as if he needed to do something to help him think. "An American? Barnes dealt with a few of them."

"Felicia said Constable something, or something Sheriff. Like that."

Hickie's frown disappeared. "Marshall Brown. Oh yes, I know all about him."

"Give me a description."

"Let's see. Southerner, late fifties, aggressive and ingratiating. He's in the demolition business. Wanted Barnes to throw in with him. Brown thought Barnes' local contacts could be useful. I don't think Barnes was very interested, but he saw quite a bit of Brown at one time."

"Did he like him?"

"I'm not sure." Hickie laughed. "They went clay pigeon shooting one time and Barnes nearly got shot. I remember that. Some kind of accident. He joked about it."

"How do I get in touch with Mr. Brown?"

Hickie got up and opened a filing cabinet. "Must be something on him. Yes, here we are. Brown & Brown. Office and plant in St. Peters . . . ah . . . Ashley Road. What's your interest?"

I copied the phone number and address from the letterhead he showed me into my notebook, and shrugged. "Nothing to it, probably. Just something to check."

"How's Felicia?"

"She's fine. Could you get cracking on O'Fearna now and give me a bit of a rundown on the business stuff, say tomorrow?"

"I'll try."

That was fair enough. There was no reason why he should reorder his life for me.

* * *

It was early in the afternoon and the day was fine. I could have gone calling on Marshall Brown. I could have found out some more about Todd's violently disposed competitor Riley, and paid him a visit. I could have gone through my police contacts to get a registered owner for the car whose number plate I sort of knew. Instead, I went to Redfern. I got no answer to my knock at the house in Chalmers Street, but the big windows to the upstairs balcony were standing open and I had the feeling that Felicia Todd wasn't far away.

I found her in the park. She was sitting on the grass in the shade of a poplar tree and she was sketching a corner of the park and the street and houses beyond. I came up quietly and stood, not wanting to break her concentration. After a few minutes she stopped making rapid passes across the paper, looked up and saw me.

"Hello," she said. "Stay there and I'll draw you."

"Come on. Don't waste the charcoal."

"Don't move!"

I stood on the grass, feeling like a fool and admiring the curve of her neck and the sureness of her movements. She pushed up the sleeves of her blue-and-white-striped shirt and sketched fast, shooting occasional quick glances at me. She was wearing a blue skirt, long and flowing, and sandals with leather ties that wrapped around her ankles. Her hair was nut brown in the sunlight and her skin was tanned. It was the first time I had seen her in natural light, and it seemed to give her an extra vitality. I was pleased to see that she had a camera on a strap around her neck. She finished with a flourish.

"Come and have a look," she said. "Don't pretend you're not curious."

I walked across and looked at the pad. She'd made me look every day of my age and hard and stern, like an exacting athletics coach who expects his charges to do better.

"Christ," I said. "Is that how you see me?"

I held out my left hand and helped her up from the grass.

"That's the exterior impression," she said. "I'd have to sit you down in a good light and take some time to get the inner Hardy."

"God forbid. I can see you've got the skills, though. If I put that on my office wall, I could up my fees."

She laughed and dropped her charcoal stick into a pocket of her skirt. We walked towards the fountain; she carried the sketch pad and a paperback book. I reached for her free hand and she let me take it. I'd forgotten the bandage and winced when her hand went round it. She let go quickly. "What's this?"

"Tell you later. Would you like to go for a drink or something?"

She stopped and I stopped. Her book hit the cement path. We were kissing before either of us knew what was happening. It seemed like years instead of months since I'd had a woman that close to me, and I felt a surge of pent-up energy. We pressed close and hard, mouths and bodies; the camera pressed sharply and uncomfortably into my chest, but it didn't matter.

She broke away and stepped back. "God," she said. "Can you come back to the studio now?"

"Yes." I picked up the book. It was Robert Hughes' *The Fatal Shore*. I carried it in my wounded hand as we hurried through the park. My good left hand gripped her right. She took a key from her skirt and opened the door. We ran up the stairs and we were both breathless by the time we stood by the bed. The breeze through the open windows was moving the curtains and the turned-back covers.

She unbuttoned her shirt and I touched her small, firm breasts. She undid my belt.

"You're doing all the work," I said.

"Shut up," she hissed. "Kiss them!"

I bent and kissed her nipples, which became hard. Her skirt

had an elastic top; I pulled it down and put my hand inside her pants.

"Everything off," she said. "Everything!"

We stripped and began a slow exploration of each other's bodies, holding back and delaying until the first of the strangeness of it was over and the excitement caused us to hurry. I had forgotten how strong a woman could be, how firmly arms and legs could grip and how solid a body could be when you drove into it, urgently and full of need.

When we finished the bed was a mess, with the sheet and blanket on the floor and two of the pillows under Felicia's hips. We moved apart and I shoved the pillows into place under our heads, hooked the sheet up over us and held her in my arms. She moved easily and loosely with me, as if we'd been doing this for years.

"Oh, that was good!" She wriggled her head free and looked at me. "I could draw you better now."

"Some parts, anyway."

She snuggled back. "If you're married or living with someone don't tell me yet."

At this point, in the past, I'd had to lie or fudge it. Not now. "I'm not. I was divorced more than ten years ago, and I haven't lived with anyone for . . . about a year."

"Over it, are you?"

"Yes."

"Have you ever had a lover die on you?"

"No."

"It's different from an affair ending. Worse in some ways, of course, but different."

"Are you saying you feel unfaithful?"

"A bit like that, but not really. It's all right. I'm glad you knew Barnes. I'm bound to talk about him."

"Bound to. So am I."

She moved away and sat up with the sheet pulled up around her shoulders. "It's bizarre, isn't it?"

"It doesn't have to be. Not if we don't let it."

"Not just a quick fuck for you, then?"

I reached up and pulled her down gently. "No. Nothing like that, Fel."

"Good. Let me up. I'm going to make coffee." She found her striped shirt on the floor and put it on; she gathered up two empty coffee mugs, both from the same side of the bed, and went out. It wasn't a bad room to be post-coital in—low bed, polished floor, clothes in those white wire Swedish drawers, and some framed drawings on the walls. There were no male clothes or items around. Paperbacks lay around the bed in piles—mysteries, poetry, travel—but books are gender-neutral.

Felicia came back with the coffee and we sat on the bed and drank it and didn't say anything. I looked at the drawings—nude studies, front and back, male and female.

She saw me looking. "Barnes," she said.

I nodded.

"I cleaned all his clothes out, shoes and that." She wept then, long and hard, with her body shaking and the grief buffeting her, until she was drained and quiet. I sat close to her on the bed, sharing the space but not touching her while she went through it. At last she pulled up a bit of the pale yellow sheet and wiped her eyes. A lot of black stuff came off on the sheet, and I realised that eyeliner was the only make-up she wore.

"Okay?"

"Yes," she said. "I'm . . ."

"Don't say sorry. It's all right. You'll miss him and things about him for years, probably. I still miss Cyn, sometimes."

"Cyn?"

"My wife. Someone else's wife for ten years or more, but still . . ."

I put my arm around her shoulders and she relaxed against me. "And who was it a year ago?"

"Helen."

"D'you miss them all, Cliff?"

"There aren't many." I pointed to the bean bag and the cane chair and the wicker chair on the balcony. I patted the bed. "We wouldn't need many more seats than this for my roll call. A few, but . . ."

She laughed. "I know what you mean. They're always with you if you let them, but they don't have to be."

"Right."

She took my right hand. "You haven't told me about this."

I told her what had happened in Coogee. She got off the bed and straightened one of the pictures on the wall. "What do they *want*, for Christ's sake?"

I shrugged. "Barnes' paintings? Documents?"

"I don't know anything about any documents. The paintings and photographs're with a friend in Bulli. I've been thinking about them. I'm going to go down and get them. I'll offer them to Piers Lang for an exhibition."

"Who's he?"

"Leon Willowsmith's arch-enemy."

"Sounds good to me. I'm waiting for everything—for O'Fear's release, for Anna Carboni, for Michael Hickie to fill me in on some business matters. I want to talk to the Bulli cops and some witnesses. Can I come with you to the coast?"

"Is it just business?"

"No." I put my hands on her smooth shoulders and she came back onto the bed, and we did some of the same things and some new things, and it was even better the second time.

13

We ate and drank whatever was in the fridge. Felicia touched up her drawings and developed some of her pictures in a darkroom that was part of the flat's second bedroom. I dipped into Robert Hughes and wondered whether I was related to the old lag Henry Hale, who arrived on the Third Fleet and endured the hell of Toongabbie. My maternal grandfather had been a Hale. I praised the photographs, which seemed to capture every detail of the park and add something to them. Perhaps Felicia's grief. But we spent most of the time together in bed.

At nine o'clock the next morning we were on the road to the south coast. I was wearing the clothes I'd worn the day before; but I keep a towel and swimming trunks, a sweater, shorts, thongs and sneakers and a jacket in the car, so I wasn't ill-equipped for the trip. I had my Autobank card and my answering machine was switched on. I had the device to monitor it sitting in the glove box of the Falcon, about ten centimetres from the Smith & Wesson .38. I had a woman who made me laugh and felt like a friend and a lover and a sparring partner. What the hell else did I need?

It was a grey but not threatening day. I'd done work in Wollongong and Port Kembla and some of the farther-flung south coast towns before, but some years back. I thought I was familiar with the route, but Felicia had to jog my memory at a couple of the turns and bypasses.

"Did you know D. H. Lawrence lived in Thirroul for a while?" Felicia said as we went into the National Park.

"I saw the film."

We talked about the film of *Kangaroo* and related matters all the way over the Audley crossing and past the turnoffs to Maianbar and Bundeena. On the other side of the park the sky seemed to clear; a couple of hang-gliders hovered, high above the coast from Otford Heights.

"Things I've yet to do," I said. "That and scuba diving."

"What about parachuting?"

"I've done that in the army."

"How was it?"

I looked at the hang-gliders; one of them executed a turn and swoop, and soared far out over the sea. "Not much fun."

"Do you find your work fun, Cliff? All this questioning and digging into lives and pushing people around?"

"No," I said. "I like the blondes and brunettes."

She looked out the window, and I felt the chill.

"Sorry. That was dumb. There isn't much of those things you mentioned. Just now and then. Mostly it's dull routine stuff. I don't mind it—I'm independent, I can think my own thoughts."

"Mm. This is awkward, isn't it? You screwing the widow in the case. Ever done this before?"

"Come on, Fel. You're not the widow in the case to me. That's not how it is. You're you, I'm me, Barnes was Barnes, the job's the job. Things can be kept separate."

"Can they?"

"Look, I know a guy who married three sisters. Three. The first one died and the second marriage didn't work out because she left him. He's been with the third sister for fifteen years. He told me that when he thinks about it, he never thinks of them as sisters. They're individuals."

She smiled. "That's a nice story."

"It's true."

"I don't care whether it's true or not. It's a nice story."

The temperature was more pleasant for the rest of the drive.

The Todds' holiday house was a 1930s-style, double-fronted weatherboard bungalow, on a bluff about a hundred metres back from the ocean. I carried Felicia's overnight bag through the rather gloomy passage to the back of the house. The light was held out by bamboo blinds drawn down low on all windows. When Felicia lifted the blinds I saw that the view of the water was a bit blocked by trees and other houses, but there was more than a glimpse.

"When can I see Lawrence's ghost?"

She pointed out the window at a narrow stretch of rocky beach at the bottom of a steep path. "Down there at high tide. Or is it low tide? I forget."

I put the plastic shopping bag that held my few possessions on the floor and moved quietly around the big room. It ran the width of the house. The room had a closed-up, musty smell. It occurred to me that this was probably her first visit since Barnes' death. We both felt the awkwardness. In holiday houses people have fun, drink and eat a bit, spend a lot of time in bed and forget their cares. That's what those places are for. We were both wondering if the mood was transferable.

"I think I'll do some drawing," she said.

I nodded. "I'll go into Bulli and poke around."

"We're well back from the scarp here. It stays warmer later. It'd be good to have a swim around four."

It was just past eleven. She was giving me my marching orders for five hours while she dealt with her memories and emotions.

"Right," I said. I kissed her on the forehead. "What provisions should I get?"

"Nothing. I'll take a walk to the shops. If you want Drambuie or something exotic you'd better get it yourself. Jesus!"

"What?"

She had opened a door that led to a narrow passage and out onto the deck that ran along the back of the house. The intense light outside showed where the door to the deck had been jemmied open and later pushed back into the frame.

"Have a look around," I said. "See if anything's been disturbed."

I went out onto the deck. An agile person could have reached it easily from the overgrown garden. Behind the house was a narrow lane and the backs and sides of other houses. No problem. The surf crashed on the beach around the headland. Felicia had taken off her sandals and I didn't hear her on the deck until she was beside me.

"Someone's been through the place," she said. "Nothing taken, nothing damaged. I suppose they're going through the Redfern flat right now. Unwrapping the tampons. What *is* this, Cliff? What's it all about?"

"I don't know. You'd better come with me."

"No chance. This is my house and I'm staying here." She stalked away and when I went back into the house I found her clicking bullets into the magazine of a .22 repeating rifle.

"Hey. What're you doing?"

"Go and earn your money, Cliff. Don't worry, I know how to use this. I'll be all right."

"Those things're illegal now. Don't you read the papers?"

"I don't give a bugger. This government's on the way out.

Bloody fools. They can't enforce that law. Every country cop's got a couple of guns himself. It's madness."

A gun lobbyist, for God's sake. I left.

Sergeant Trevor Anderson wasn't a whole lot of help. He was youngish for his rank, anxious to please but new in the district and very light on for experience.

"I don't think I can add anything to what you already know, Mr. Hardy," he said. "There were a couple of witnesses or people on the scene pretty quickly. You've got their names."

"Yes. Was there any other traffic on the road?"

He pushed back his sandy hair, which was a bit longer than normal for a cop. He also wore spectacles. It looked as if he was hoping to rise to Commissioner by force of intellect. He checked his notes carefully. "Apparently not."

"What does that mean, Sergeant?"

"None of the witnesses mentioned any. Is that all, Mr. Hardy? I've got work to do."

Merv Simpson, one of the firefighters, was at home. He had recently been laid off from a coalmine and he was happy to pass the time of day. Trouble was, he couldn't tell me anything. He had seen the fire, not the accident, and he was sure that Clarrie Bent, who had helped him, was in the same boat.

"Talk to Warren," he said. "Warren Bradley. He got us on the blower. Poor bugger sits up all night. He mighta seen a bit more."

Warren Bradley's wife read my card carefully, studied my face, and then showed me through to the back verandah of the house, which was in a bushy setting back from the steeply descending road. Bradley was a heavy-set, middle-aged man with grey hair and a pale, pudgy face that looked as if it had once been tanned and hard. He was sitting in a wheelchair, staring out over the treetops towards the water.

"Be patient with him," Mrs. Bradley whispered. "He's a bit difficult."

"I'm not bloody difficult, Mildred," Bradley said, "and I can hear your whispers a hundred yards away. Who's this?"

I went up to him and stuck out my hand. "Name's Cliff Hardy, Mr. Bradley. I want to have a few words with you about the accident on the Pass a few months back."

Bradley shook my hand. His palm was soft but there was strength in his grip. " 'Bout time someone did that. Take a seat."

I sat on a straight-backed chair beside him. Mrs. Bradley hovered. She was a thin, nervous woman who looked as if she had never known the right thing to do.

"What about a couple of beers, Mildred?" Bradley said.

"Do you think you should, dear?"

"Yes. I think I should. Stop worrying, love. The money's due any day."

"It's not the money. It's your health."

Bradley let out a bellow of laughter; his big, deep chest gave the sound resonance and volume. "My health! Just get us a drink, there's a good girl."

She left the verandah, closing the screen door quietly behind her. Bradley slapped the tops of his thighs. "Mine accident," he said. "Both legs buggered for good. Compo's coming through, but."

I nodded. "No hope?" I said. "Physio? Operation?"

"Stuffed," he said. "Mind you, I miss the fishing more than the bloody work. What d'you want to talk about?"

"Sounded to me like you wanted to talk."

"Yeah. Well, I was in a shitty mood back then. Having a bad time with all this." He touched his legs again. "Couldn't sleep. I wasn't what you'd call co-operative. I was giving Mildred a bad time. Everybody."

Mrs. Bradley came back with a tray on which were four cans of Fosters, two elaborately shaped glasses, and a bowl of peanuts.

"Good on you," Bradley said. "Do you, mate?"

"Yes," I said. "Thanks. What about you, Mrs. Bradley? Are you having a drink?"

She smiled, shook her head, and drifted away.

"Never touches it," Bradley said. He popped two cans and pushed one towards me. He poured a little beer into one of the glasses, swilled it around, and drank it. Then he took a pull from the can. "Can't stand those bloody glasses, but it's not worth the trouble to say so. Cheers."

I repeated his manoeuvre and took a swig of the cold beer. Fosters isn't my favourite, but it was my first drink of the day, which helped it along. "I got the feeling Sergeant Anderson didn't have too many clues."

Bradley snorted. He took a handful of peanuts and put them in his mouth. He chewed and spoke around them. "Doesn't know his arse from his elbow. Sent some kid of a constable up here to talk to me the day after. Bugger that."

"What did you see, Mr. Bradley?"

Bradley drained his can in two massive swallows and popped another. "I've thought about it a bit. It's hard to be sure. I'd had a few." He tilted the can. "And I'm on these painkillers—make me pretty woozy sometimes."

"But it was two A.M. on a good, clear night."

"Yeah. You seem a reasonable sort of a bloke. What were you before you got into this game? Not a copper?"

"No. Soldier, timber worker, insurance investigator."

Bradley nodded approvingly. "I reckon he was run off the road."

I drank some more beer and took a sidelong look at him. He didn't have the appearance of a fantasist or self-dramatiser. Bitter, but who wouldn't be? "Go on," I said.

"It's hard to be sure. Take a look. The trees block the road a bit."

I leaned forward and looked. The drop made the distance hard to judge, but the road couldn't have been more than a hundred metres away and the view was mostly clear. "Where did he go over?"

Bradley took more nuts, chewed noisily, and pointed.

A clear stretch went into a wicked bend. A section of the metal siding marking the edge of the shoulder was freshly painted. The trees fringed the road before and beyond the place on which his finger was trained.

"It's partly a feeling," Bradley said. "Or I might have just heard it. I dunno. But I think there was another car or a four-wheel drive . . . a truck or something, real close . . . too close. And it kept on going."

"And you didn't tell the police?"

"Like I say, I was pissed off with them." He drank deeply. "I phoned Merv Simpson and Clarrie Bent, and they got down there with the extinguishers and the bags pretty smart. I done my duty."

"Right." The beer was warming up in my hand and not tasting so good, but I drank some more. "Did you hear him brake or did he go straight over? Was he skidding? What happened?"

"Bloody mess," Bradley said. "Straight over, but there was stuff flying everywhere—barrier posts, branches, you know? Door wide open . . . Look, you haven't had any nuts. D'you want this other beer?"

It wasn't something to take back in triumph to Felicia, but I felt a degree of satisfaction. Something was happening *now*—the surveillance and break-ins—and this was the first clue that something had happened *then*. I negotiated the steep roads above Bulli carefully and rejoined Lawrence Hargrave Drive for the drive back to Thirroul. Coal trucks used to hammer along these roads to the risk of everyone else on them, but they're much quieter now. Good for drivers, bad for the area. The sun was dropping below the scarp, cooling the day down fast. The sea sparkled but there was a brown smudge on the horizon where the pollution drifting down from Sydney meets that coming up from Wollongong. Nowhere's perfect.

I ran the Falcon through the gates Felicia had opened and parked beside the house. She came to the front door minus the .22 and seemed pleased to see me. We kissed. She had been shopping. We had a beer and ate grilled fish and salad. She had been to the local library, seen a few acquaintances in the street. Nothing unusual had happened. She seemed tense, though.

"I have to collect the pictures tomorrow," she said. "I don't want anything to happen to them. I'm nervous about it."

"I'll be there. Stopping things from happening's supposed to be my forte. It'll be all right."

We went for a walk on the beach, drank coffee on the deck, and went to bed. I had my pistol in its holster rolled up inside my beach towel. She put the .22 under the bed. We laughed about that and were tender with each other. I was pulled from a deep sleep by the insistent bell of the phone. It was 3 A.M. and the phone was nearest to my side of the bed. I hesitated about answering it, and Felicia reached across me.

"Yes? Michael? Yes, he's here."

She passed the phone to me.

"Hardy," Michael Hickie said, "hope this isn't awkward for you."

"It's all right, Michael. What's up?"

"It's O'Fearna. He's been stabbed."

14

Hickie was pretty excited. When he'd calmed down, he told me that he'd started to make the moves to get bail for O'Fear. He hadn't encountered any serious problems and he had expected his release that day.

"That is today, you understand? It's today now."

"I understand. What happened?"

"He got knifed late last night. It happened in one of the recreation areas, I understand. I got the message around eleven. It's taken me a while to locate you."

I didn't ask him how he had managed to do that. "Where is he, and how is he?"

"He's in the prison hospital. He's going to be all right, but it was a serious attack. Apparently O'Fearna's tough and quick. The point is, he can get out today, and he wants to see you very badly. He says you've got a lot to talk about."

"Is he safe where he is?"

"I spoke to him on the phone very briefly. He says he's safe. But he wants you to pick him up tomorrow afternoon."

"When's that?"

"Two o'clock. At the Bay."

"I'll be there."

"He said you would be."

I thanked Hickie and hung up. Felicia had gone off to make tea. She came back with a tray; I dipped the bag in the water until the liquid was black and sipped it. It tasted like burnt stringybark, but I was able to get some of it down. I told Felicia about O'Fear.

"What does it mean?"

"I'm not sure. But something's happening." I told her what I had learned the day before about the way Barnes' car had left the Bulli Pass road. She sipped her tea and had difficulty in swallowing. "Poor Barnes," she said. "Why didn't he confide in me?"

"Either he wasn't sure about the threat and didn't want to alarm you unnecessarily, or it was too dangerous."

"Bloody men. Always sure they can handle it. Are you the same?"

"Try me."

"I want to stay here for a bit. I wanted it to be with you, but if you can't stay that doesn't change anything."

"I don't think you should."

"There you are. You want to protect me, is that it?"

I nodded.

"I don't want to be protected. Just take a look at yourself." She touched my nose and put her index finger on two scars—one on my arm and one on the shoulder. "What are they?"

I shrugged. "From football."

"Rubbish. Gun or knife wounds. You can scarcely look after yourself." She was looking at me fiercely. Suddenly she grinned and kissed me. "It's all right. I don't really mean you're incompetent or anything, I'm just making a point. I want to live my own life."

"I don't want to stop you, Fel. I just . . ."

"Shh. You want to haul me back to Sydney and stick me away somewhere I don't want to be. No way. Look, let's be logical. You can take the paintings to Sydney and deliver them to Piers Lang. He'll tell *everyone* he's got them. So that should take care of any threat from that direction. Right?"

"I suppose."

"And if all this searching *isn't* for the paintings, then they've looked through my knickers enough now to know that I haven't got anything they want. Doesn't that make sense?"

"Maybe, but I'd feel better . . ."

"There it is! *You'd* feel better. I'd feel worse. I'm staying."

In the morning we drove to a house in Austinmer and loaded up with Barnes Todd's paintings and photographs. They filled the boot and the back seat. There were also several boxes and thick folders full of sketches and photographs. Felicia's friend Deborah was a big, overall-wearing woman, who had built her own house and earned her living by landscape gardening and doing building jobs for others. Her hobby was sculpture and, from the way she strode about carrying pictures and boxes, I had the feeling that she'd do big ones. I would have felt happier if Deborah could have taken up temporary residence with Felicia in Thirroul, or vice versa, but it was worth more than my life to say so.

Deborah's voice rumbled like a coal loader. "I'll run her back in the truck."

"Okay," I said. "I'll ring you tonight, Fel."

Felicia bent down to the driver's window. She kissed me and touched my bristled chin. "Why don't you grow a beard? Might suit you."

I took the freeway back to the Princes Highway and was unloading the masterpieces at Piers Lang's gallery in Riley Street, Surry Hills, not much more than an hour after leaving Austinmer. For long stretches of the drive I had forgotten that I was carrying items that could be worth millions of dollars. I don't think I believed it anyhow, not on the word of Leon Willowsmith. The gallery assistant who was helping me unload missed his footing and dropped one of the folders of photographs. The string around it snapped and the contents spilled across the floor. I collected the pictures together and saw enough to note the sharp clarity of the shots—you could see the veins of the leaves on the trees, or convince yourself you could.

The assistant relieved me of the folder and dusted the glossy black and white surfaces with his handkerchief.

"Marvellous," he said. He held up one of the framed photographs and looked at it as if he had been waiting for it all his life.

I got a detailed receipt from Lang, a rolypoly little man who seemed wildly enthusiastic about everything. The atmosphere at Lang's place was completely different from Willowsmith's. Here there was a stronger smell of paint than of money.

"Leon Willowsmith's not going to be too keen on this," I said. "Maybe you should beef up your security."

"Good idea," Lang said. "Are you in that business?"

"Sort of."

"Would you be interested? God, those photographs."

I was folding the receipt, ready to leave, but something in his voice stopped me. "What about the paintings? I thought . . ."

"The paintings are good, too."

I tried to look as if I knew what he was talking about. He beckoned me into his office—a small room cluttered with paintings, photographs, and objects that could have been pieces of sculpture or plastic bottles that had been left in a hot oven. "This is sensational stuff," Lang said. "Potentially."

I nodded.

"I think Felicia and I have an understanding. Are you in her confidence, Mr. Hardy?"

"Up to a point."

"Tell her everything will be all right and that I'll make sure the catalogue appears exactly as she wants it to. Now, as to the matter of security . . ."

"You'll have to tell me a bit more about your understanding with Mrs. Todd. She's a subtle woman. If I'm going to be involved at the security end I'll need to know any . . . angles."

Lang passed his hand over the thin dark hair on his rather pointy head. "Well," he said, "maybe I should protect myself. I'm not going into this thing with my eyes shut, you know."

"What thing, Mr. Lang?"

"Did you know Todd? Like him?"

"I knew him slightly. He was okay."

"Do you think he was honest?"

"More or less."

"Exactly. He was certainly smart. You don't think the photographs are his work, do you?"

I tried to remember whether Felicia had actually said so. I couldn't recall. "I assumed it."

"Exactly. So will everyone else, and the catalogue will confirm it."

"Are you saying he didn't take the photographs?"

Lang gave me a level look. "Did I say that?"

"Whose work are they?"

"Who do you think? I've said enough. This is all very delicate. What about the security?"

I told him I wouldn't handle it, but I gave him the name of a firm I occasionally deal with. I didn't think it would hurt to stay in some kind of touch with the snaps and daubings.

* * *

O'Fear eased himself gently into the car. He was wearing a grey suit that was slightly too big for him. He had lost weight in gaol. I put his bag in the back, but I didn't open any doors for him or offer other help. He would probably have broken my arm.

"How bad is it?" I said.

"Could be worse. Glanced off a rib. A dozen stitches and no ballet dancing for a while."

"Where d'you want to go?"

"Where does anyone want to go after a period of durance vile? To a bloody pub, boyo. Have you got a shooter?"

I nodded and started the car. We drove to a pub in Chifley near the Star drive-in theatre. It was showing a couple of the Harrison Ford Indiana Jones movies and I wondered who would want to go to drive-ins any more, now that we had videos and all-night TV. Unless it was for the same old reason.

The pub was undergoing a refit and only the saloon bar was open. There was no draught Guinness, so O'Fear accepted a bottle of Sheaf stout. He filled a schooner expertly and drank it down in a couple of long gulps. I had a middy of the same stuff in lieu of lunch.

O'Fear wiped his mouth with the back of his hand, refilled his glass, and signalled for another bottle. "Ah, that's better."

"You're not going to tell me you went all those months without a drink. I could smell it on you the other day."

"It's not the same." We were sitting on bar stools. O'Fear pushed some of the change from my ten bucks across the bar and the barman replaced the empty bottle with a full one. He took some money and put back very little. The walls of the bar were covered with photographs and paintings of cars and horses. I didn't think Felicia would approve too much of my spending her money in here.

The barman put a clean glass in front of him and O'Fear ignored it. "Bloody prat," he said, "I like to stick to the same glass." He drank deeply. "This has the breath of freedom in it.

Well, Hardy, you almost got me killed, so when arc we going to start talking money?"

"Eh?"

"This has got to be big. I'm inside there, cruisin' along and mindin' me own business. Me only worry is that I haven't seen me boy Danny for a bit. Come to think of it, I could've hired you to look about for him. Anyhow, one fine day I talk to you, and the bail's up and some bastard sticks me. Now, it was worth somebody's while to do that, so it has to be worth my while to put me life in hazard."

"Christ, what do you want? I got you out, didn't I? That's my own money I put up."

"So it is. And you'll get it back when I stand trial. What would you say to a fifty-fifty split?"

"I'd say no."

"If I go to Tasmania you'll lose the lot. I hear the folk scene's still very big down there."

"You wouldn't be hard to find."

"But think of the expense. Come on, boy, you want to know what happened to Todd, don't you?"

"Do *you* know?"

"I can help you find out. Now, don't be mercenary about this. We're in the same boat."

"How's that?"

He finished his drink and licked froth from his lips. He belched deeply. "Honour demands that you complete the job and commonsense demands that you be paid for it. I need the money too, and by Christ my honour's at stake."

He poured another schooner full and I let him top up my middy. It had been a long time since I'd drunk stout and I wasn't sure I still liked it. I thought I could probably acquire the taste again. O'Fear sipped at the froth and grinned at me. "It's grand for the pain."

"I'm curious about your honour."

All the lilt and blarney were suddenly gone from his voice. "No one puts a knife in Kevin O'Fearna and walks around to boast about it. Have we got a deal?"

I thought about it while another mouthful of stout went down. O'Fear was no one's idea of a perfect partner. He was reckless, he had a bad temper, and he got too drunk too often. On the other hand, if it came to a fight there was no one better to have on your side. And a feeling was growing inside me that this was getting bigger than a one-man job. I had the beginnings of some plans—trap setting and such—all of which would require manpower.

"I don't know whether to be flattered by your enthusiasm or overwhelmed by your generosity," O'Fear said.

"I'm being realistic," I lied. "Maybe you don't know anything at all, at all."

"I know something. But I don't know enough to make sense of it."

"What about your own case? Could this be related in any way?"

He hesitated, but only for a split second. "I think not. It's my opinion that little matter'll take care of itself."

I told him about the searches of Todd's houses and Warren Bradley's suspicions regarding the way Todd's car had left the road. He nodded and touched his side tenderly. "Like I said, something serious."

The drink had relaxed me; I was musing now. I allowed myself a thought I wouldn't have entertained before my conversation with Piers Lang: *Maybe Todd was blackmailing somebody.* But I said, "Somebody's looking for something Todd had. What would it be? Evidence of some kind. If Todd had evidence, why didn't he do something with it?"

"You know the answer to that."

My mood was almost philosophical now. "Yeah. He couldn't trust the cops."

"Or didn't know which ones to trust. He might have made enquiries though. And where one person can enquire, another can enquire too."

"You should have been a lawyer, O'Fear. A judge. Instead of a dumb mick brick-shifter."

"I've met a few judges. I can't say that I liked them much."

"You'd better tell me what you know. And for five thousand dollars, it better be good."

He grabbed my hand and pumped it, which hurt me and must have hurt him too. We were a couple of minor casualties. "We'll make a great team, Cliff. But can I tell you something?"

"What?"

"You could do with a shave."

15

I thought the first problem would be to get him out of the pub. I didn't want to start off with a boozy ramble about this and that, in which the connections were apparent only to minds leached by alcohol. I was wrong. He came willingly, without even finishing his third schooner and leaving a good bit in the bottle. We drove to Maroubra, my old stamping ground, where the memories are fading as the landscape changes; most of the shops where we bought the sweets that ruined our teeth are gone, and parts of the beachfront have had more facelifts than Liz Taylor. But the sand and water do not change and we sat in the car and looked down at the pool and up and out into infinity.

"A fine place," O'Fear said.

"Where I grew up." I pointed to a kid on a surfboard, bobbing out beyond the breakers. "That's me, thirty years ago, when I wasn't delivering papers or cutting the grass or sneaking a smoke behind the dunny."

"I knew Barnes Todd longer than that," O'Fear said. "You knew we met in Korea?"

I nodded.

"We stayed in touch, more or less. Two wild men, you know what I mean? Well, we'd have a few jars and a natter. Barnes got me out of several little bits of trouble from time to time, and I'd return the favour."

"How?"

"There's a deal of sabotage in truckin'. I cracked a few skulls when it got tried on."

"Did Barnes do any sabotaging of his own?"

"By way of reprisal, yes."

"Shit." I watched the surfer get up gracefully as the wave took him. He powered along with it, sweeping across its face and turning sharply to get the force behind him for the run to the beach. "He could've had a hundred enemies."

"He could. But there was one in particular."

I swivelled in my seat and looked at O'Fear. It was warm in the car and sweat was trickling from his hairline towards his eyebrows. Suddenly he was nervous. I looked around us; no other cars parked nearby and a clear view in all directions. "There's no one around," I said. "You can talk."

"I was remembering the night," he said softly. "I have to admit I was scared, although devil a thing really happened."

The dramatic tone irritated me. "If this is blarney, O'Fear, I'll . . ."

"This is straight goods! He had me driving around to all manner of places. I didn't know where I was half the time. The whole of the bloody city we were covering."

"What was the purpose?"

"I'm buggered if I know. He'd have me wait near the car while he sneaked off somewhere. He was taking photographs, that I know for sure. Had this bloody great camera around his neck."

"What sorts of places?"

"I'm not sure."

"Don't go coy on me."

"Be buggered. I was taking a drop or two at the time. From me flask. Well, it was all so bloody boring. I can drive like Stirling Moss no matter how pissed I get. I can drive all right, but I couldn't always swear to where I am."

"You're a disgrace. Go on."

"Well, he'd hop back into the car and give me a grin, and it'd be off to the next place. But one night it was different."

"When was this?"

He moved slightly, easing the wounded side. "I'm talking about the last time I saw him. Let's see, that was about two weeks before he died, or a bit less. I'm not certain. I don't keep a bloody diary, you know."

"When did you go inside?"

"A couple of days after the night I'm talking about. I was bashed, of course, and I've had a lot on me mind. You'll have to understand if I'm a bit muzzy on the details."

I took out my notebook. "Don't worry, I'll pull you up if you get too vague. Go on."

"This place I'm talking about. It was big, I know that, because he had me drive around the area a few times. Around the streets. I only caught a glimpse of the place itself. Look, I'll admit I'm confused. I don't where the bloody hell it was."

It was rare for O'Fear to admit that he didn't know something. A sign of truth? "Get on with it," I said.

"Barnes was being extra cautious. He was dressed like a burglar, soft-soled shoes an' all. And he had a gun as well as his camera. I didn't like it. I tried to persuade him to take me along, but he laughed at me. Would you believe it? He had a thermos of coffee with him. Told me to drink it and sober up."

"Did you?"

"I drank it, but I spiked it from the flask."

"You must have *some* idea of where you were?"

"Oh, sure. Between the bloody Blue Mountains and the sea." Either the calming effect of the alcohol was wearing off or the memory he was about to dredge up was difficult for him. He looked at me testily. "D'you want to hear this or not?"

I nodded.

Sweat was standing out on his forehead. I got some tissues from the glove box and he dabbed at his face. "Thanks. Barnes was away longer than usual. M' nerves were on edge what with one thing and another. He came running back—first time I'd seen that. He had this bundle with him."

"What sort of bundle?"

"One of those big plastic garbage bags. He shoved it in the back seat and told me to get moving as quick as I could. I did it, too."

"Hang on. This bundle—heavy or light?"

"Pretty heavy. He had to lift it, like."

"Did it make a noise?"

He strained to remember, failed and became angry. "What is this? The bloody secret sound?"

"All right. Then what happened?"

"I drove off but I was pissed. After a bit Barnes drove. I went to sleep in the car and woke up when we got back to his place in Botany. He paid me, called a taxi and I went home."

"You don't know what happened to the bag?"

He shook his head. "I let him down. I swore I never would again, but I never got another chance." He looked at me; sweat had plastered the red hair to his scalp and his collar was a rag. Anyone else in that condition might look defeated, but O'Fear looked ready to start a fight. "I'd like to help now, and that's not the booze or anything else talking."

"I don't quite understand why this rocked you so much, O'Fear. I mean, it sounds a bit toey, and you were pissed, but . . ."

"I'll tell you. It wasn't any of that rattled me. I've done more than my share of scary things at night. It was this—Barnes Todd was scared that night. Did you ever see him scared?"

I found it hard to even imagine. "No."

"Nor me. I saw him in Korea, remember. Bloody millions of Chinks around all tryin' to kill us, and it was like a day at the races to him. It was him being afraid that scared me."

I had been making notes, preparing to haul O'Fear back from fantasy or evasion, but his account was coherent enough. "How many places did you go to that night?"

"Two or three."

"What was the usual number?"

"It varied. Sometimes only a few, sometimes a hell of a lot."

"Did Barnes have a list or a chart of some kind?"

He considered the question and I was convinced that he was making a genuine effort at recall. Eventually he shook his head and then tapped his temple. "No. He had it all inside."

I looked at my notes and wondered what to make of O'Fear's story. Nothing came.

"He must've had some name for what you were doing. What did he call this midnight rambling?"

"Reconnaissance."

The surfer I had watched before was back out in the deep water again. The wave rose and he was up, balanced and forceful; crouched, driving the board, he resembled a powerful machine, perfectly designed for the job it was doing. "What sort of car did you drive on these reccies?" I asked.

"A Ford Laser. Barnes had a small fleet of them at Botany."

"Mulholland, you black bastard." O'Fear and Bob Mulholland shaped up and exchanged mock punches. O'Fear's left jab was just a sketch, and he kept his damaged side protected.

"You didn't tell me you knew this lunatic, Cliff," Mulholland said.

"I was trying to forget it. I've just bailed him out of gaol."

"That's right! Tell the world me life story."

"Calm down, O'Fear." Mulholland prodded O'Fear's belly. "Prison's done you good."

"Prison never did anyone any good," O'Fear growled. "You remember when I was drivin' for Barnes?"

Mulholland nodded. "I remember the dings you put in the cars." He stopped when he saw me looking at Anna Carboni's empty chair with the dead screen in front of it. "Oh, Cliff, I left a message on your machine. Anna's been sick for a couple of days. You'll have to wait for that work."

"Nothing serious, I hope an' pray?" O'Fear said.

"Gastro, or something like that. From the wog tucker, I expect."

O'Fear waved a finger at him. "Prejudice."

"When you two get through with your routine," I said, "maybe I can do some work. I might not need all the details now, Bob. I think we have a closer focus on the problem. That's if this bloody Irishman can remember where he was on a certain night."

Mulholland looked puzzled and O'Fear gave him a wink. "He owes me money. Makes him testy. Are you goin' to look at the car?"

It was difficult to stay annoyed with O'Fear for long. "I am that," I said. "Can we take a look at the Lasers, Bob?"

Mulholland pointed to three sets of keys hanging on hooks near the door. A truck roared into the yard and I heard shouting. "I'm pretty busy," Mulholland said. "Do you . . . ?"

"Go on," I said. "We'll try to keep out of your hair."

He strode to the window of the office and gesticulated at the truck driver. O'Fear and I went out and walked towards the part

of the yard where the Lasers were parked. We had to wait for
two trucks to back past us towards the loading bays.

"Busy around here," O'Fear said.

I told him about Felicia Todd's decision to keep Barnes Enterprises afloat. He glanced at me slyly.

"Ah," he said, "a woman in the case. And you have an eye for
her."

I ignored that. We reached the cars and I tossed a set of keys
to O'Fear. "I don't suppose you know which one you drove?"

"I'd say I drove them all at different times."

"We won't find anything, but let's take a look."

"It's only right," O'Fear said.

We searched the cars thoroughly. The only thing of interest I
found was a crumpled sheet of paper ruled up into columns with
a space for headings. "What would you say this is?"

O'Fear, the old truckie, had no doubt. "A log sheet."

Back in the office, we found Bob Mulholland elbow-deep in
paperwork and close to bad-tempered. I put the keys back on the
hooks. "Sorry to interrupt again, Bob."

Mulholland grunted.

"Trouble?"

"A bit. Riley again, and others."

I turned to O'Fear. "Do you know this Riley character?"

"I do."

"Could it have been something to do with him that night?"

O'Fear shook his head. "Wasn't his place, at least. I'd know
that joint drunk or sober from some earlier doin's Barnes 'n'
me'd had there."

Mulholland tapped a pencil impatiently on the desk.

It had been a fairly long day with a few miles covered and
many words spoken. I could have worked up a bit of impatience
myself, but I held it in check. "Could I have a look at the log
sheets for the Lasers, Bob?"

He pointed to a stack of thick loose-leaf binders. I flicked through the top sheets in the first binder. The logs showed times, mileage, fuel costs. I patted Anna's desk and beckoned to O'Fear. "Job for you, mate. I want you to sort through these. Do every car. See if you can isolate the night in question and work out the radius of the area you travelled. Know what I mean?"

"Jesus," O'Fear said. "Do I have to?"

I slapped him on the shoulder and he winced. "Sorry. I think it's a good idea. Might jog your memory."

"And what'll you be doin'?"

"Checking on a demolitions man named Brown in St. Peters. Think you could've been in St. Peters that night?"

O'Fear shrugged. "A heavenly name for a hellish spot. Shouldn't we be conducting a big search for the photographs and the bag?" O'Fear retained the "g" in upmarket words like "conducting."

"Tomorrow. Have you got somewhere to stay tonight?"

O'Fear had taken off his jacket and hung it over the back of Anna's chair. He had the stack of binders in front of him and was clicking a ballpoint pen he'd taken from his pocket. He gave me one of his ingenuous smiles. "I thought perhaps your place, Cliff."

I reminded him of the address and told him where the spare key is hidden. "Will you be all right?"

"Is there drink in the house?"

I said there was.

"Then I'll be fine. If I can't make me way from Botany to Glebe, then it's time I retired." He clicked his pen. "I'm not too keen on this, though. I'm a man of action."

"We need a man of brains just now."

"Well, after all, I'm a graduate of Trinity."

Mulholland looked up. "What pub's that?"

O'Fear opened a folder. "I won't be disturbin' your good lady, then?"

"You remember my wife, O'Fear. The blonde architect? She left ten years ago."

"She was never the woman for you, Cliff."

I still had the log sheet in my hand. I crumpled it and threw it into a wastepaper bin. "Her sentiments exactly," I said.

16

Since small business people started installing answering machines, Commander phones, and car phones, I've almost given up ringing to arrange appointments. There are too many ways they can duck you. A direct approach is best; most people aren't rude, most are curious. It was late in the afternoon when I arrived in St. Peters. Ashley Road was a non-descript thoroughfare, half given over to factories and half to houses that looked as if they had been squeezed onto blocks of land that were too small for them.

Brown & Brown presented a long, high brick fence to the street. I could see the superstructure of a couple of cranes and bits of earth-moving equipment poking up into the sky, and the outlines of some buildings that would not have carpet on the floors or paintings on the walls. I parked further down the street and walked back to give myself some time to rehearse what I was going to say. I had it worked out by the time I reached the wide main gate. Brown & Brown looked to be doing pretty well. Tyre tracks on the road and drive showed that a lot of traffic had passed through the gate. The brick wall was new. Reddish-brown stains on the cement marked where water had run for years down a rusty tin fence and across the footpath.

A smaller gate further along from the main entrance was set in a recess in the wall; it even had a skimpy overhanging roof. I pressed the buzzer and looked around for the closed-circuit TV lens, but the door swung open before I found it. I went up a cement driveway towards an office building that had a small flagpole standing outside it. The U.S. and Australian flags hung listlessly from the mast. I went through double doors into a functional reception area where posters and photographs on the walls showed the sort of work Brown & Brown did. Brick towers were shown crumbling under the force of explosions; giant steel balls reduced brick walls to rubble. The man at the desk was about thirty; he had a tanned face and a mass of wrinkles around his eyes, as if he spent a lot of time squinting in bright sunlight. Big shoulders and neck, cropped brown hair.

"Can I help you, sir?"

I gave him my card. "I'd like to see Mr. Marshall Brown."

He read the card and looked at me with interest. "Private detective, eh? Don't think I ever met one before. Hold on, I did run into one when we were wrecking the brickworks."

"What did you run into him with?"

He smiled, showing teeth not as white as those of the workers in the posters. "He was from an insurance company." He looked down at a typed list on the desk. "I think Mr. Brown has all the insurance he needs, if that's . . ."

"It's not," I said. "Just for interest, if you wrecked a brickworks, what're you doing here?"

"Mr. Brown thinks everyone should know every part of the business. I'm on a two-week stint here. After that I do vehicle maintenance. Then I can get back to the bulldozer. Have I been polite?"

"Very," I said.

"Mr. Brown says we should be polite. What's your business?"

"I'll be polite too. Please tell Mr. Brown I want to talk to him about Barnes Todd."

He made a note on a pad and then his big fingers with their blunt, broken but very clean nails punched buttons on the intercom system. I heard an American voice respond: "Yes, Wayne."

Wayne? I thought. With luck, his surname.

"A Mr. Hardy here, Mr. Brown. A private . . . investigator. He says he wants to talk to you about Todd Barnes."

"Barnes Todd," I said.

Wayne corrected himself. "Barnes Todd."

There was a pause. Then the American voice again: "Show him in, Wayne."

Wayne pointed to a door which had an exit sign over it.

"Exit?" I said.

"A joke of Mr. Brown's. Just go through, Mr. Hardy." I was three steps towards the door before he added, "Nice to meet you." At least he didn't say anything about spending a pleasant twenty-four hours.

The room was as functional as the space outside. Big desk, a couple of chairs, low table, bookshelves, and filing cabinets. Papers, maps, and blueprints were spread or stacked on every surface. Marshall Brown was standing behind his desk; he didn't wear a string tie or a jacket with piping on it, or cowboy boots. He wore a white shirt, dark tie and trousers and he was as bald as an egg. He was about five foot six, ten or more years older than me, and the pale skin on his face sagged around his jawline. He gave me a quick, moist handshake.

"Sit down, Mr. Hardy." His voice was high and light. I'm no expert on American accents. Southern, Hickie had said. Well, he certainly wasn't from Boston or New York.

I sat, and he looked at me for a full half minute.

"I think I'm a pretty fair judge of a man," he said, "if you say you're a private eye, I'd be inclined to believe you. But I'd check up before I told you anything."

I put my licence folder on the desk. "What would you do before you gave me any money?"

His laugh was a high whinnying sound. He glanced at the licence and pushed it. "I'd double-check. You mentioned Barnes Todd."

"You knew he was dead?"

"Yeah. I should've sent a wreath, but . . ." He waved his hand at the paperwork.

"It was 'no flowers,' anyway."

"Uh huh. Well?"

I hesitated, playing the part of a plain man searching for the right words. "I was in Korea with Barnes," I said. "Me and a few others thought we'd like to chip in for some kind of memorial. You know, a plaque or something like that."

"Is that so? How's his widow feel about it?"

It was a God-will-strike-you-dead kind of question. And if God wouldn't, Felicia would. "She's agreeable. You were in Korea, weren't you, Mr. Brown?"

"U.S. Infantry. Second Division." There was a snap in the words and his jaw seemed to tighten. "How about you?"

"Sergeant, A Company, Third Battalion."

"I was a captain, most of the time."

"Barnes was . . ."

"One of the toughest soldiers I ever saw. It was a bloody terrible war. Best forgotten."

"Can you forget it?"

His eyes moved around the room without focusing, as if he wasn't seeing the furniture and the blueprints but something else —paddy fields, burning tanks, panic-stricken men about to die? "No, I sure can't," he said quietly.

"Did you and Barnes talk much about Korea?"

"Yeah. We talked. But about business, mainly." He undid the

top button of his shirt and loosened his tie. Flesh bulged. "I guess I could make a contribution. It's the least I can do."

"What d'you mean?"

He looked at his watch. "I usually work for another hour, but what the hell. Got anything you need to do just now, Mr. Hardy?"

He seemed to be two people—the flabby, harassed business-man and the steely cold warrior. Both could be dangerous and I felt very unsure about him. "I'm free for a while," I said cautiously.

He got up and walked across the room; his jacket hung on a key sticking out of a filing cabinet. He freed the jacket, turned the key in the lock, and put it in his pocket. "Let me take you somewhere."

We went out through the foyer and Brown made a sign to Wayne with his fist and forefinger. Wayne nodded.

"What's that mean?" I said.

"Dozer driver stuff. Means cut off the motor."

We left the building and got into Brown's Volvo, which was parked in a slot labelled "the boss."

Brown snapped his seat belt on. "Safest car on the market. What d'you drive?"

"A Falcon."

He didn't comment. He drove out through a boom gate at the back of the big yard. Shadows were spreading across the cranes and other equipment, which were painted dark green and looked like prehistoric monsters immobilised by a climatic change. Brown drove aggressively but well. I wondered whether he had a gun in the car, the way I did in mine. Great help it was to me there. If he had headed for the river or anything that looked like a dumping ground, I suppose I would have got ready to jump him or jump out, but he didn't. He worked his way across to Newtown and parked in a side street near St. Stephen's church.

It was after six o'clock, but King Street was still crowded and the shops were open. I hadn't seen a paper or heard a radio for days and had lost track of the week. It was Thursday—late-night shopping. The road was full of cars crawling along and spewing fumes, but no one seemed to mind. If you can't take car fumes, you don't live or shop in Newtown. Brown was a quick walker; his purposefulness cut a path through the strolling shoppers and I recalled reading somewhere that this was a characteristic of successful Americans—purposefulness. I was finding it irritating.

"Where the hell are we going?"

"You'll see."

Brown cut across the path of a woman pushing a laden shopping trolley and pushed open a door. I followed him into a long, dark room. Some soft music was playing and, as my eyes adjusted to the concealed lighting, I saw several low tables with cushions laid out geometrically around them.

Brown's nostrils flared. "Smell that."

I sniffed. I could smell seafood, spices, sesame seeds, chilli.

"This is the best Korean restaurant south of Seoul," Brown said.

A waiter came out of the nether darkness and, after a lot of hand-shaking and bowing and Korean palaver, we sat on cushions with our legs under us or under the table. The dishes started to arrive and Brown identified them for me. *Ku-jeol-pan* came in a box with compartments that held fish, meat and vegetables, and small pancakes; *kimche* was a very hot pickled cabbage; *nakgibokeum* was braised octopus with spicy sauce. Brown ate quickly but delicately; I picked along in his wake. We drank Korean beer from green bottles.

"Barnes and me came here all the time," Brown said. "We'd eat this great food and get high on the beer and talk about old times."

"The war?"

"Sure. What else?"

"Bob Mulholland told me about an accident you had when you were clay shooting with Barnes."

Brown gulped beer and speared up some *kimche*. He chewed it with relish. A few strands of the stuff had nearly taken the lining off my mouth. "Yeah, yeah, that's right. Damn careless. But there was no harm done. Were you at the Han?"

I didn't answer. I was still unsure of him, but getting surer. A few more customers had arrived and soft conversation blended with the clink of bowls and glasses. The waiter brought more beer.

"They bring it till you tell them to stop," Brown said.

I drank some beer and told him that the closest I'd ever been to Korea was Malaya. I told him Bob Mulholland's story about the U.S. captain and his threat to Barnes.

"You thought I might be him?"

I shrugged. "I think Barnes was murdered. It was something I had to check."

Brown went on eating for a while. He drank more beer and belched. "I know all about that, but I never thought I'd have to talk about it."

"I think you have to now, Mr. Brown."

"Yeah, well, he's dead. What harm can it do? There haven't been any real war heroes for a long time."

I said nothing and waited for him to order his thoughts and memories. When he spoke, he sounded much older than the go-get-'em businessman, much more tired. "The sergeant got it wrong, Hardy. I was there. The sergeant couldn't see a thing and Barnes 'n me stage-managed it all. What could we do? It was get down that fuckin' road or die."

"What happened?"

Brown looked around him as if the walls might become his accusers. He guzzled a glass of beer and shook his head. "We shot people to get through. All kinds of people. You had to be there to know what it was like. The panic was like . . . like cancer racing through everyone. Someone had to do something. We weren't the only ones."

"What about the American captain?"

Brown sighed. "That guy was a coward. He kept going in the space we opened up. Bleating about human rights the whole fuckin' time. Shit, the Chinks would've cut off his human rights where his legs met. The top brass wouldn't have understood. No one who wasn't there could understand. We did what we had to do."

I had had enough military experience to know what he meant. "A scapegoat?"

Brown nodded. "The guy was courtmartialled. He died in Leavenworth pretty quick. Cancer, I think."

My image of Barnes Todd was in fragments, although I knew that was a naive reaction. I couldn't find any words. I drank some of the tepid beer.

"What can I say?" Brown growled. "It was a shitty war. Everyone who died in it was just plain dumb."

I knew he was talking a kind of brutal, pragmatic sense. Despite what the promoters and medal-givers say, the main thing about war for the participants is survival. I tried to concentrate on my reason for seeking Brown out in the first place. I located it finally among the ruins of my stupid illusions. I gave him a quick résumé of the case as I understood it. "So forget history," I said. "Any clues on why anyone'd want to kill Todd?"

Brown had listened attentively. He shook his head. "Can't help you, I'm afraid. On the business level, all I know is I wanted Barnes to come in with me. He wouldn't. No hard feelings. We met, we ate, we drank, we talked about the good times. That's all."

"I see."

He gave me one of his hard, tight-jawed looks. "That's not a

bad idea about the memorial, though. Why don't we do some
thing about that?"

I nodded.

"Have some more *kimche,*" Brown said.

17

Marshall Brown paid the bill. He drove me back to my car and wished me luck. I watched the Volvo until it turned at the end of the street. Brown had handled himself well; if he was lying he was the greatest actor since Olivier. I sat in my car with the thin beer and the exotic food inside me and ruminated: here I was, slightly dyspeptic, fairly sure that a flawed man had been murdered, sexually involved with that man's wife, and teamed up with a gaolbird who could be playing some weird Irish game of his own. It's a strange way to make a living. I was aware of one big consolation, however—I was thinking less and less about Helen Broadway and all that pain.

I didn't want to go back to Glebe just yet, either to wait for O'Fear or to find him already there with a bottle and the blarney. Suddenly my mood changed—maybe it was the *nakgibokeum.* In fact, I told myself, I was doing pretty well on this job, complications aside. I had eliminated the American captain and probably the threat-from-the-art-world theory. The danger to Barnes Todd had come from whatever he had been doing on his nocturnal perambulations with O'Fear. And there was physical evidence of that—photographs and something heavy in a plastic garbage bag. Those things were still being looked for by the opposition, and so could be found. I stared through the windscreen, which had picked up some salt from the spray at Maroubra. I saw fences and buildings and roofs stretching away forever. A set of photographs and a gar-bag suddenly didn't seem so easy to find.

I started the car and drove without purpose. It was almost dark and I switched the lights on automatically, checked the rear vision mirror for a tail, automatically. I found myself heading for Bondi, drawn towards the sea, as almost everyone is if they've ever lived near it for a significant period of time. I cruised down Hastings Parade and parked outside the building where I could live and work, mortgage-free, if I chose to do so. It was part of the estate of a grateful client from the past, now dead. The heirs were still grateful, and I could have the place for a song. It was white, freshly painted. I couldn't see the water from the street, but I knew that all of the windows along one side of the apartment afforded an eyeful of the Pacific.

This wasn't sleazy, beachfront Bondi; this was a land where exterior woodwork was painted every year, two videos per household territory, compact disc country—suburbia-by-the-sea. *Do you really want to live and work here, out of the smog?* I thought. Where the kids are bright and helpful instead of drug-dulled and suspicious? Where the sun in the morning looks fresh and clean? Where the people who haven't got money on their minds aren't likely to last for long? I still didn't know. If I didn't decide soon, the opportunity would evaporate, and maybe that would be the best thing. I kissed goodbye for now to my personal shot at paradise, drove away, and stopped near an all-night chemist with an orange phone. There was a bottle shop a little further along and I bought a six-pack of Swan Light so that I could get a fistful of change and have something to do with my hands when I phoned Felicia Todd in Thirroul.

She answered, sounding relaxed and pleased to hear from me. I told her I'd delivered the paintings and that I had eliminated the Korean connection.

"That's a relief," she said. "And what has this Irishman told you?"

"It'd take too long to go into but I'll fill you in when I can. In the meantime, do you know anything about a set of photographs Barnes took? A special set, relating to his business?" As soon as the words were out I realised that I could be on tricky ground, if what Piers Lang had said was true.

Felicia's reply came slowly. "No. The only photographs I know about are those you delivered to Piers Lang."

"Had you looked through them? Were they all . . . ?"

"Yes. All subjects, if you know what that means. I've almost finished classifying them and relating them to the paintings. They're not at all to do with trucks or storage or bloody security."

"What about a big plastic garbage bag? Heavy."

"I don't understand."

"Did you see Barnes with such a thing? Hiding it, maybe, or doing something unusual?"

"I only ever saw him put garbage bags out the front of the house. Cliff, what is this?"

"Evidence. Never mind."

"When will I see you?"

"When are you coming back?"

"I'm not sure."

That was pretty clear. She was leaving it to me. Her tone was welcoming, though, and I felt encouraged. "I'll keep in touch and get back as soon as I can."

"Good. I hope that's soon. Deborah's staying the night and

she's brought her dog along. With the stabbing on top of the housebreaking, I'm not feeling as confident as I made out."

I rang off after telling her I thought it would be sorted out soon, which was more optimistic than truthful. But I was intrigued, which is a way of being optimistic.

There's a bolt on the inside of the front door of my house. It had been thrown and my key wouldn't open the door.

"Who?" The voice was soft, immediately behind the door.

"Hardy, who else? O'Fear?"

The bolt was drawn and the door opened quietly. O'Fear eased himself out and beckoned for me to move into the shadow at the front of the house, where the wistaria hangs down from the top balcony. He was white-faced, moving stiffly, and carrying a gun.

"What's happened to you?"

"To me? Nothing. But this idiot followed my cab from Botany to your place. I spotted him in the first half mile. He came in with a shooter and I had to tap him on the head. I hurt my side a bit doin' it."

"What idiot?"

"He's inside. A young feller, maybe about thirty, with a twelve-year-old brain."

"Unconscious?"

"He was. He'll be comin' out of it soon. I can hit so as to knock you out for a precise time, y'see. This was a half-hour tap at the most. I allowed for his size."

As always with O'Fear, it was difficult to tell truth from bullshit, but there was no doubt that he was an expert in violence. My first thought was that we had a hostage.

"I was thinkin' you might make a few private enquiries of him," O'Fear said, "although he looks like a tough little nut.

Perhaps I should do it mcsclf. I'm rathcr tirin' of these fellers havin' a go at me."

"That's brilliant. What're we going to do? Torture him?"

"I wasn't thinkin' of bribing him with my share of your ill-gotten gains, I can tell you that!"

"Perhaps it's to do with your other trouble?"

O'Fear shook his head. "That hasn't the mileage in it. It's not a shootin' matter at all. No, it's to do with Todd all right. Look, Cliff, he'll be stirrin'. I put him in your little falling-down bathroom . . ."

From the back of the house came the sound of glass breaking.

O'Fear waved the gun. "Christ, he'll be out and away."

I shattered the existing record for getting from my front door into my car. I drove to the end of the street, turned through the new block of flats, and stopped on the rise. If he went over the back fence he had to come out down the street from where I was. It would take him a few minutes to negotiate the fences and gardens, but he would come. There was no other way.

I was right. He dropped over a fence onto the pavement about the same time as a car drove up the street in my direction. He was a small man, dressed in dark clothes but with a white stripe on his jacket sleeves. He shrank back against the fence as the car went past. Then he ran.

I drifted down the street, keeping well back and not showing any lights. He rounded the corner into Glebe Point Road and sprinted down the hill towards the water. I saw him take the turn into the avenue beside the park before I put my lights on and followed. I picked him up under the light where the street bends. He tore open the door of a car, gunned the motor, and took off. I kept as far behind as I could, delaying on the turns and hugging the kerb until he was back on the main road. I relaxed a little then, allowed a car to pass me to serve as cover, and tried to pick out something distinctive about the car I was following. There was nothing distinctive, no broken tail light or racing stripe, but the number plate was KNM 223.

He drove badly. His reactions were slow and he was indecisive; probably the results of O'Fear's gentle tap. But he managed to get into King Street and turn off towards Erskineville. This was harder for me—narrow streets, some of them one-way, relatively unknown territory. He threaded through between the factories and terrace houses and dark, empty looking lots, still driving erratically, clipping the footpath more than once. His right indicator flashed and he turned sharply into a wide concrete driveway. A man stepped out of a lighted booth, consulted something the driver showed him, and waved the car ahead. A heavy metal gate slid open, and KNM 223 was home at last.

I pulled in to the kerb and killed my lights. It was a long, narrow street, poorly lit. The side I was parked on was mostly taken up by the backs of factories. Opposite me and a bit further on, the metal gate was set in a high brick fence. Higher than that of Brown & Brown, almost prison-like. I felt in the shelf under the dashboard and located the half bottle of rum I keep there for emergencies. Emergencies are fairly few and the bottle was almost full. I took a swig and looked at the brick fence. The guy in the glass booth was bent over, reading or eating or playing with himself. Anyway, he wasn't looking at me. I took another drink and squinted until I shut out the peripheral light and could read the words painted on the gate: ATHENA SECURITY LTD.

I let out a rummy breath in a low whistle. Athena was a big security firm, comparatively new. It advertised extensively and aggressively and boasted that it had the latest technology in all departments of the game. I get a lot of the security business propaganda in the mail—brochures, magazines, sales pitches—and Athena had loomed large in the material in recent times. It's a very competitive field. I glance at the stuff, some of it I file, most of it I throw away, but one unusual fact about Athena had stuck in my mind—the head of the company was a woman.

18

I drove around the Athena establishment, taking in the high walls, signs of electronic equipment, and the glow that suggested spotlights within. The wall was lower along one side which occupied a section of a neater residential street. It was almost as if Athena didn't want to look too institutional among the tidied-up terraces and wide bungalows. Image is everything, or nearly everything. Still, it wasn't the sort of place you storm with a Smith & Wesson .38 shouting: "Freeze! Nobody moves until I get some answers to these questions."

The rum was warm and comforting inside me as I drove home. I was looking forward to some coffee and plain food. I'd even be able to manage a conversation with O'Fear now that we had something solid to talk about. It was good to make a connection. I could check out Athena and its boss lady, talk to everyone all over again from this new angle. What might Anna Carboni and Bob Mulholland know? I remembered Mulholland saying Barnes Todd was considering moving into the security business.

All very promising. And the cut on my hand had stopped throbbing.

I parked in the street behind mine, put the .38 in my pocket, and approached the house warily. No sense in taking chances now that things were starting to break. I hoped O'Fear had not found the scotch or had brought his own. A few lights were on, as per normal. Nothing was lurking in the shadows. I opened the door and stepped in with the gun in my hand and knowledge of the terrain on my side. The house was quiet. I walked right through it, upstairs and down. There were no gunmen or baseball bat swingers. No obscene messages scrawled on the walls. There was no sign of O'Fear either.

A soggy, bloodied-up towel was lying in the bath. The louvre window was a wreck, and there was blood on the floor and outside on the bricks. Look for a small man—and he had to be small to get through the window—bleeding from the hands and head. I cleaned the bathroom roughly, threw the towel in the laundry basket along with my own shirt and underwear, and had a shower. I kept the .38 within reach and, as I washed, I tried to remember when I had last used it. *Some time ago*, I thought. Good. Keep it that way.

I sat down with a strong black coffee and my notebook and reviewed the day's confusing developments. O'Fear had gone voluntarily; there was no evidence of a struggle, and he would have managed to leave some sort of sign even if they had caught him unawares and marched him out. But no note either. Gone where, with whom? My supposed ally, who also represented $10,000 on the hoof, was wandering about with a knife wound in his side, doing God knows what and in possession of a pistol.

Added to that, I had the new information on Barnes Todd—art charlatan with his wife's connivance, and war criminal. I felt in less than complete control of the situation.

* * *

I got to the office early and rummaged through my files for material on Athena Security Ltd. I had kept a coloured brochure and a form letter suggesting that independent enquiry agents should consider amalgamating with bigger concerns. I had written something rude across the letter. The managing director's signature at the bottom was a big, bold scrawl—Eleni Marinos. There was a postage-stamp-sized photograph of her beside the letterhead. She had pale skin, blonde hair, and light eyes and looked about as Greek as Grace Kelly.

According to the brochure, Athena was the "newest, most innovative security firm in the Southern Hemisphere." It could supply guards, patrols, and electronic protection. It had an armed delivery division, a strongbox deposit facility, and a security courier service. It could provide enquiry agents, bodyguards, drivers, pilots, and debugging experts. Paranoia Paradise. A close and productive relationship with the state and federal police was implied, along with the certainty of insurance cover and legal advisers of an eminence it would be too vulgar to detail.

I looked at the cool, calculating face of Ms. Marinos and wondered. I was sure I had seen her in the flesh, but I couldn't pinpoint the memory. I occasionally went to the functions thrown by the various arms of the security business. At them I had encountered some sharp minds and classy talkers, although after a while the display of, and concentration on, money tended to depress me. Anyway, the roll-up was overwhelmingly male, and Eleni Marinos would have stood out like a diamond in a dustbin. She didn't look the type to walk her dog in Jubilee Park or drink in the Toxteth. She wouldn't exactly fit in at the Journalists' Club, where I occasionally went with Harry Tickener. I had never met her—I'd have remembered the name—but I had seen her. Where?

I used the Birko to make instant coffee. I had some instant Turkish I'd been meaning to try and this seemed as good a time as any. I poured the boiling water over the pulverised grounds

and obeyed the instructions by adding some sugar. I stirred the
cup with a spoon that Helen had lifted from a cafe in Darlinghurst after becoming exasperated at the lousy coffee and in-
flated prices. I sipped the thick, sweetish brew and, the way a
smell or a sound can, the unusual taste triggered the memory. I'd
seen Eleni Marinos in a Greek restaurant. Her escort at the time
had been Barnes Todd.

I couldn't remember exactly when it was. More than a year,
because I'd been with Helen. We both liked Greek food and this
place in Paddington was our favourite. We had been to a film,
and the hour was late. Barnes was just leaving and I hadn't even
had a chance to speak to him. But that's where I had seen her—
across a smoky room. I remembered her white skin standing out
amid the general swarthiness, and the way she had tossed her
blonde hair as she said something to a waiter. In Greek, presum-
ably. Then she had clasped Barnes' arm and they had gone out.

I stared at the letter and the brochure as I tried to make
something out of it. The brochure carried a picture of one of the
silver armoured cars that had appeared on the streets in the last
few years. They carried a big green "A" on the sides and inspired
confidence. The guards wore silver jackets, which the men in the
game I knew—ex-cops, ex-soldiers, ex-footballers—wouldn't
have liked. But maybe they had a new breed of armed guard
these days. Maybe they were art school graduates or had degrees
in communications. All the more reason not to amalgamate.

I phoned Barnes Enterprises and got Anna Carboni.

"You're better?" I said.

She sniffed. "No, but I'm back. I'm glad you called. Bob said
you mightn't be needing that work I was going to do after all."

"Yeah, sorry, that's right. Sorry to deprive you of the overtime."

"Don't worry. I need the time in bed more than the money
right now. Does that mean you know what happened to Mr.
Todd?"

"Not really. Is Bob there?"

I waited, fiddling with the new dressing on my cut hand. The cut had healed well. I tried some more of the coffee and couldn't decide whether I liked it or not. When Mulholland came on the line, I asked him if O'Fear had been there that day.

"No," he said. "I understood he was going to your place last night. What's up?"

"Nothing. I've . . . lost track of him. Did he get anywhere with those logs?"

"He said it must've been a pretty tight run. Fifteen to twenty kilometres the round trip."

"Anything else?"

"No. Hold on . . . Anna's waving at me." I pushed the coffee aside. "She's miffed," Mulholland said. "She reckons he made a hell of a mess searching the office."

"But did he find anything?"

"I don't know."

"Did he take anything away with him?"

"Look, brother, I was busy. He called a cab. Said he was going to your place. He went. I wasn't keeping tabs on him. I just don't know."

"Okay, I'm sorry. I know you're busy, Bob. A couple more questions. Did Barnes ever have any dealings with Athena Security?"

"I think so. I don't know the details. Michael Hickie'd know more about it."

"Right. What about Eleni Marinos? Did Barnes ever mention her?"

Mulholland said the name and there was a pause. I heard muttering. When he spoke again his tone was cautious, guarded. "Anna tells me he knew her before he was married," he said.

"Knew her?"

Mulholland's voice was thick with impatience. "Sometimes I

wonder how you gubbas ever got past the Blue Mountains. Barnes and Eleni Marinos had an affair. Serious, Anna says."

Michael Hickie's secretary, Jenny, was still in a job. She told me that Hickie had gone to play touch football.

"It's the middle of the morning on a working day," I said.

She giggled. "That's when they do it. Michael . . . Mr. Hickie, and some of his friends. He calls it, ah . . . rebellion as relaxation."

"Where do they play?"

"Waverley Park. I'm sure you'd be welcome. They're always looking for extra players."

It had rained overnight and the morning was fresh and clear. The traffic moved well along Bondi Road, and I had no trouble locating the cluster of professional men's cars near a corner of the park. Out on the grass a group of men huddled, broke apart, ran, jumped, and fell. I parked, walked closer, and Hickie spotted me.

He waved. "Hey, hey, Hardy. We're a man short. Want a game?"

I was wearing jeans and sneakers and a clean white shirt, but I had an old T-shirt in the car. The players wore shorts and rugby shirts, tracksuit pants and singlets. I looked them over carefully —no giants or obvious psychopaths. I signalled "Yes" to Hickie, jogged back to my car, and changed.

The next forty-five minutes I spent throwing and running and slipping over on the damp turf and laughing. It was a good-natured game among men who were past their physical best but not giving up without a struggle. They ran hard; some of the body contact was accidental, but not all of it. I was faster than a few, heavier than a few others, and I held as many passes as I dropped. Hickie and I were playing on opposite sides and we had one heavyish collision. I thought he could have avoided me, but he didn't, and he came off slightly second best. No ill-feeling. I finished the game well and truly winded, mostly as a result of a last mad dash, and with a slightly bruised shoulder despite the soft going. I remembered games I had played as a kid—under blazing skies on grounds baked rock hard, and in blizzards and ankle-deep mud. They were tough games—I've still got a scar where some teeth went through my right ear. Back then, as kids, we were proving something to the world. Now we were mostly proving things to ourselves.

After the whistle, Hickie introduced me properly to the men who had been Dave, Ben, Russ, etc., for the purposes of the game. They smiled and wiped away sweat and most of them drove off, but Ben produced a cold six-pack of Heineken, and we leaned on the bonnet of his Celica for a spot of mateship.

"Ben's a surgeon," Hickie said.

I recalled Ben's precise throwing and catching.

"You've got the hands and eyes for it," I said.

Ben tilted his bottle. "Yep. Long may they last."

The other stayer, whose name I didn't catch, tossed his empty at Ben, who plucked it out of the air effortlessly. "See you," he said.

We chatted while Ben drank the spare bottle. After he'd gone I wiped myself off with the T-shirt. Hickie was tossing the ball from hand to hand.

"You didn't come here to play football," he said.

"No, but it was fun. I've got questions."

We squatted on the grass.

"Have you seen or heard from O'Fear since yesterday?"

"No."

"What d'you know about Barnes' dealing with Athena Security?"

Hickie wiped sweat from his face and drank from his bottle. Ben had had two, mine was long gone, but he still had an inch or more left. "That's a bit tortuous. Athena's a strange concern, a bit mysterious. They approached Barnes for an investment, then for his custom, and eventually made him a takeover offer."

"How did he react?"

"He considered the investment and using their services. Then he had ideas of going into security himself, so he backed off. He had a high opinion of their operation, though."

"What about the takeover?"

"I think he'd sooner have lost a leg."

"Do you know anything about Barnes' relationship with Eleni Marinos?"

Hickie nodded and finished his beer. "It was a very hot affair. Before he met Felicia, but not long before. I don't know the details but Barnes ended it. It was a very rough patch for him. He drank a good bit and . . . you know . . ."

Of course I knew. Anybody who had been through the relationship mill knew only too well. The indecision, the resolutions, and the turnings-back. Sheer hell and we keep on doing it because, as Woody Allen says in *Annie Hall,* we need the eggs. Lucky are those who don't need the eggs. Or maybe they're not lucky. I helped Hickie tidy up the bottles and the cardboard wrapper and the soft drink cans. We stowed the rubbish in a bin and stood together, looking across the grass in the direction of the sea.

"How're things with Felicia?" Hickie asked. He rubbed his shoulder, which must have been sore from our hard bump.

"She's still at the coast. I haven't got any good news for her." I didn't tell him about the new slant I had got on Todd from Piers Lang and Marshall Brown, but I did tell him about the attack on O'Fear, and how I had established the connection to Athena Security.

"Well, I can see how Eleni Marinos' nose would be out of joint," Hickie said. "Barnes had really knocked her back. But to kill him?" He shook his head.

"Must be more to it than that," I said. "I've got a terrible feeling that O'Fear is on to something and going it alone. I admit I don't know what to do about Athena, but I doubt he has any better ideas."

"I could look through the correspondence—see if I can come up with something."

"That'd be good. Thanks." As he spoke I realised that a question had been nagging at me since early in the case. After the break-ins at Coogee and Thirroul, why hadn't the searchers done the obvious thing and looked through Michael Hickie's files? As I chewed on the thought, Hickie opened the driver's door of his yellow Datsun 200B. I could see that the door had been panel-beaten and resprayed. I pointed to the new work.

"What happened?"

"I got rammed a few weeks back. It's been in the workshop for ages."

That figures, I thought. Hickie was thinking too. He got into the car and wound down his window, as if to invite my next question.

"Tell me," I said. "Who handles the security for your office building?"

Hickie clicked his tongue. "Athena," he said.

19

My thoughts were uncomfortable. Felicia Todd was involved in a deception about Todd's creativity. She had scores to settle and there might be justifications for it. But I was worried that she might know something about Barnes' dealings with Eleni Marinos and Athena, and be holding out on me. It was tricky territory. In my experience, men can talk about their present partner's ex-partners without distress, but women find it difficult. I don't know exactly why this is; perhaps because women like to work things through and, by definition, they cannot work through relationships they haven't been in. I wanted to see Felicia, and advance our budding love affair, if that's what it was, and this topic wasn't calculated to help. It was a new slant on conflict of interest.

I went home and packed a bag, drew out some money, and filled the Falcon's tank. I set off for Thirroul with two guns and not many ideas. In Rockdale I waited at the lights alongside an Athena armoured van. The large driver wore aviator glasses and had silver insignia on the epaulettes of his shirt. He read a copy of Evan Whitton's *Can of Worms* while he waited. He chewed gum, too. With operatives like that available, I wondered why they would employ a little runt like the one who had broken my bathroom window. Then I remembered his neat driving the night he had followed me, and his quick recovery from O'Fear's "little tap." Maybe his gun hadn't been loaded; maybe he was a master of restraint.

I got to Thirroul around three. A battered Holden ute was parked in the Todd driveway and a big German shepherd greeted me at the gate.

"Easy," I said. "Friend of your owner's friend."

The dog barked and Deborah appeared at the door. She was wearing her overalls with the bottoms tucked into football socks above dirty gym boots. "It's all right, Hero," she said.

The dog wagged its eight-pound tail. I patted its head and stepped past.

"Hero?" I said.

Deborah nodded. "Hero was a woman, didn't you know that?"

"I forgot. Well, I suppose I should've phoned, but . . ."

"What's that supposed to mean?"

"Nothing."

"If you think Felicia and me're having an affair, you're dumber than you look. Forget it. We're friends. She's straight. Got it?"

"Yes," I said. "I'm glad you're here. Some pretty strange things're happening. Where is she now?"

"Having a sleep. We talked late and had a few drinks. She's got no head, poor love. Got up for a while this morning and crashed again. She's told me a bit about what's going on." She glanced at my bag. "See you've come to stay."

"Not if she doesn't want me to."

"She will. I want to talk to you. Come around the back."

I followed her and Hero around to the back of the house. We went up the steps and took chairs on the deck. The Pacific Ocean foamed quietly on the beach a hundred metres away. I squinted and could see the dark smudges of ships strung out on the horizon. Deborah looked in the same direction.

"Strike's tying up the port," she said. "Bludging men'll be the ruin of this country."

"You're not exactly laying bricks yourself at the moment, Deb."

The rumble of her laugh was a lot louder than the waves on the beach. "I think you might be all right, Chris . . . or whatever your name is."

"Cliff," I said. "My mother wanted Errol as in Flynn, but my father wouldn't wear it."

"Thank God for that. Fel's having serious thoughts about you. She's guilty, of course, because it's not long since her husband died."

"I feel guilty about that, too."

"You shouldn't. The man was a shit. I didn't shed any bloody tears when they hosed him off the highway."

I was almost shocked; it was the third bad opinion of Barnes Todd in a row after all the glowing tributes. Deborah's viewpoint was necessarily slanted, but in the investigative business three sources amounts to confirmation. I tried to keep my voice neutral. "Why d'you say that?"

She pushed back some straggling dark hair. Hero, the dog, watched her every move and looked as if it would jump off the bluff into the sea if Deborah told it to. She smiled down at it and Hero curled into a big relaxed ball. Maybe that was what Deborah liked—attention and obedience. "Todd owned this place for years. It was pretty much of a ruin and he only got around to getting it fixed up after he married Fel. I did most of the work on it."

Things weather fast on the coast, and I hadn't noticed that

the deck and the sliding doors and the landscaped garden were newish. "That's when you met Fel?"

"Yes. I knew Todd before that. He used to bring women down here." She laughed. "Well, why not? I would, too. It's a great place."

"What're you getting at, Deborah?"

"He wasn't faithful to her. He brought a woman down here after he was married. Twice at least. I didn't give a shit at the time. No business of mine, and I've got no faith in heterosexual monogamy. I suppose she'd have done the same after a while. But it cuts me up that she regards him as a saint. She won't hear a word against him. Started out the other night talking about how nice you were and ended up crying over Todd. Bloody madness. Still, I suppose you're no prize either."

"Probably not," I said. "Look, this isn't idle curiosity. It could be important. Can you describe the woman?"

"Bottle blonde. Forty or more. A real bitch."

"Do you know her name?"

She shook her head. "Heard it, but I forget. Foreign." She heaved herself up from the deck chair, and the dog rose in a simultaneous motion. "Well, three's a crowd. I'll take off. Tell her to give me a ring."

I stood and had an impulse to shake hands, which I suppressed. "Thanks for looking after her."

She snapped her fingers, and the dog bounded down the steps. "You do the same," she said.

Inside, the house was dark and cool. I put my bag down and went through to the main bedroom. Felicia was lying on the bed in a huddle. She heard me and sat up.

"God, you gave me a fright!"

"Sorry. I should've rung but I wanted to see you, not talk to you on the phone."

She held out her arms. "I'm glad."

I went over to the bed and we reached for each other. She pulled me down and kissed me hard. She was wearing a long red T-shirt and skimpy underpants and her body felt comforting and exciting at the same time. She lifted the shirt and put my hands on her breasts.

"I like that," she said. "Oh, I like that. I got drunk last night."

"So I hear."

She jerked away. "Christ! Deborah!"

I kissed her. Her breath was a little winey but not unpleasant. I eased her pants down from her full, rounded hips. "Don't worry. She's gone."

"Let's fuck," she said.

20

I came wide awake with Warren Bradley's words sounding inside my skull: . . . *Stuff flying everywhere—barrier posts, branches, you know? Door wide open* . . . What sort of stuff? And why had the door been open?

Felicia sat up beside me. "What is it?"

I didn't answer. These sorts of insights are fragile things; they can disappear like dreams if you don't consolidate them quickly. I put my arm around Felicia's bare shoulders and held her. Our bodies were warm from the bed and the contact. She nuzzled into me, and I stroked her hair while I thought it out. *No reason for a door to fly open. The Calais might have been rammed by a heavier vehicle travelling faster, but that wouldn't do it. What if Barnes had opened the door? And thrown something out?*

"What time is it?" I said.

Felicity checked her watch. "Nearly five-thirty."

"When does it get light?"

"In about an hour. Why?"

"I have to go looking for something."

"God, are you always like this in the morning? Up and running this early? I don't think I could bear it."

I laughed and kissed her, but I got out of bed too. "No. I can sleep in with the best of them. Want some coffee?"

"Tea," she said.

I got dressed and made the drinks. She was only half awake when I brought it to her, but she made an effort to sit up and drink it. I reminded her about the evidence O'Fear had referred to—a heavy bag—and our search for it in Botany. Then I let her in on my inspiration.

"I suppose it's possible," she said. "What could be in the bag?"

I sipped my coffee. I was drinking it strong and black and it was a bit of a jolt to what had been a very relaxed system. Excitement over the chance of finding the bag made me incautious about the other matter. "No idea. Tell me, Fel, what do you know about Barnes and a woman named Eleni Marinos?"

She spilled half of her tea on the sheet. "Shit! Why do you ask me that?"

"Is that a problem for you?"

"Very much so. I don't want to hear her bloody name, much less talk about her. Is she involved in this?"

"Could be."

Her face, which had been sleepy and relaxed, went tight. I could feel waves of hostility coming from her. She mopped vigorously at the wet sheet with her T-shirt, which had been lying on the bed. "Christ, am I never going to get clear of that woman?"

Light was showing at the bottom of the half-drawn blind and the birds were starting up in the trees. It should have been a good day for us, but suddenly it wasn't.

I touched her shoulder. "I'm sorry, love. I should have felt around it a bit more first before opening my big mouth."

"Bullshit! That's bullshit! I'm not a child. I can face facts. I bet you've been talking to Deborah."

"Yes, but the name came up in Sydney first."

"I bet. Her name comes up all the bloody time. Deborah thinks I don't know about Barnes and . . . her, but I do. I did. Oh shit! Why did you have to . . . ?"

"That's the nature of this business, Fel. It often comes down to this—the awkward question, the unwelcome name."

"I suppose you're going to tell me they had a love nest in Elizabeth Bay or something?"

"No. Nothing like that. I'm really interested in the business dealings—Barnes Enterprises and Athena Security."

She shook her head miserably. "I don't know about that."

"This isn't really the time to talk about it, but I don't think you need to suffer. I don't know anything that suggests Barnes was seriously involved with Marinos after he met you. And some things point the other way."

"What do you mean, seriously?"

"Can we leave it until I get back?"

"Sure, sure. Let's leave it, period."

She flopped down on the bed and rolled over, burying her head in the pillow. I'm a combative person by nature and life and my trade have made me more so. I wanted to tell her that I knew about her deception with the photographs and paintings. If things had got sticky enough, I might even have said something about how Todd had saved his arse in Korea. But, painfully, I've learned to cut the connection between self-justification, my anger, and my vocal cords. I tiptoed out of the bedroom, which was starting to fill with light.

I got the car as close as I could to the place where Todd's Calais had gone off the road. I had to walk back through some lantana and scrub and scramble up a steepish slope to reach the actual spot. I was breathing heavily when I got there. The day was clearing fast; a little mist hung around the top of the scarp but, from this height, the ships on the horizon were sharp-etched and the headland to the south was like a giant knife blade thrusting into the sea.

Just beyond the restored section of barrier, the damage started. Some saplings had been scythed through, and the path taken by the car was visible through the undergrowth and light timber, down to the blackened area where it had burned, a hundred metres or more below the road. I tried to take a bearing from a post on the angle the car had taken. I imagined myself in the driver's seat . . . opening the door . . . throwing something out as the car lost traction and the engine screamed. Not a pleasant process. The ferns and bracken were thick and still wet from the dew. I trampled them down, wishing I'd brought a bush knife or a scrub hook.

Cars and trucks hummed on the road above me as I slowly worked my way along to the likely points of landing. I looked back and up through the misty air and could just make out the balcony of Warren Bradley's house. I adjusted a little to the left, but the first promising clump of bushes held only a couple of beer cans, thrown from vehicles. My jeans were sopping wet to the thighs and I reopened the cut on my hand bending back branches and breaking bushes. Further down the slope, the trees shut out some of the light and made the search harder. There was no way to calculate how the bag would behave. Would it rip and distribute its contents? Would it bounce?

I slogged on, bleeding, sweating, and running out of chances. The bushes became hard and spiny, the earth underfoot was soft and I was aware that I was approaching a sizable drop. The slope was gullied by run-off water that had exposed the roots of some of the bigger trees. I caught my foot in one of the roots, fell over, swore, and found the gar-bag. It was wedged in under a fallen branch; leaves and sticks and small stones carried by the run-off water had half-covered it and I had to tug it free. In so doing I ripped the plastic bag but that didn't matter because it wasn't a single bag but three or four heavy-duty jobs enclosed inside each other. The other layers had been torn in various places, but not seriously. It was tied tightly with heavy twine at the top, and whatever was inside had been well protected.

I stood with the bag in my hand, half-expecting someone to give me a round of applause. It was moderately heavy and bulky. It clinked and clunked when the contents moved inside. It didn't tick or hum, and there was no tinkle of broken glass or rustle of paper. It seemed to have something firm, like plywood or heavy cardboard, as a base. I slung it over my shoulder and worked my way back across the rough ground and up the slopes. My fall had jarred my right arm slightly and I had to hold the bag in my left. As I swapped it over, I noticed I'd got blood on it. Tampering with the evidence.

Back at the car, I opened the boot and cleared a space for the bag. The twine was thick and the knots had hardened. I cut it with a pocket knife. My burglar's kit includes a pair of rubber gloves; I pulled them on and reached into the bag. In a couple of seconds I had fifteen objects spread out in front of me: pieces of wood and pieces of metal—the stocks and lengths of the barrels of seven Winchester double-barrelled shotguns. The wood was chipped and the metal was rubbed and scratched, but the cuts were fresh. As well, there was a set of blown-up photographs enclosed between stiff cardboard and tightly sealed with heavy masking tape.

I put the stocks and barrels back in the bag and slit the tape that held the photographs together. The bag had hit hard, bounced and fallen a fair distance so that the cardboard was bent and creased. The photos likewise, but they were clear enough. The six glossy black-and-white shots had been taken at night.

They showed shadowy scenes, from slightly different angles, of men unloading objects from a van. Some of the men wore silver jackets. Some of them carried automatic rifles. The faces of several of them were plainly visible.

21

Felicia turned over the photographs, straightening and smoothing them, laying them out on the kitchen table. She glanced at me uncertainly. It didn't seem like the time to tackle the question of the authenticity of the photographs I had delivered to Piers Lang. These weren't in the same class. "Pretty rushed work," I said. "Still, some of these faces are sharp."

"Mm, some kind of infrared system," she said. "I don't know much about that sort of thing."

I pointed to one of the gun-toters, a pudgy, pale-looking individual with a vacant expression. "I feel I know this one, but I can't place him."

"Barnes was killed on account of these photographs?"

"I guess so." I opened the bag and exposed a couple of the sawn-off stocks and barrels. "And for these."

"Ugh. What are they?"

I told her, and voiced my suspicion that the guns had been shortened on the Athena Security premises. "That in itself is a very serious offence. Barnes must have got wind of it somehow and acquired this evidence."

"God," she said, "That sounds serious."

"It's dynamite. Athena's a very big business, and it's growing. The right connections, very important contracts. A thing like this could lead anywhere."

She was standing close to me and she put her hand on my arm. "I'm sorry about this morning. I haven't sorted myself out yet."

I'd been wound up tight, trying not to say the wrong thing, watching the implications of every word. Now I relaxed a bit. "It's not surprising. A hell of a lot's been happening very fast. And it's all confusing."

"Yes, it is." She dropped her hand but perhaps it didn't matter. Maybe we were on the way back to harmony. "Tell me everything," she said. "What d'you know about Barnes and Eleni Marinos?"

I retied the bag and collected the photographs. I knew I'd be spreading them out and getting tired eyes from staring at them and feeling the frustration mount as I struggled to put a name to the face. I didn't want all that to start yet. I remember thinking when I found it that the bag hadn't ticked; it was starting to tick now. "What about some breakfast?" I said.

She smiled. "You're stalling, but okay."

She cut a grapefruit and made coffee while I toasted bread and boiled the eggs. We bumped into each other moving around in the small kitchen. That was nice. We took the food out onto the deck. The sun was well up, but there was a light cloud cover and no wind. The sea was serene; a pale, rippling grey.

Clambering around on a hillside at dawn had made me hungry. I wolfed down the grapefruit. I cut an egg in half, scooped it out, and spread it on the toast. Then I shook salt and pepper over it. Felicia scowled at me.

"Too much salt. Much too much. Your arteries'll be like cement pipes."

"I gave up tobacco and cut down on alcohol," I said. "Please leave me my salt."

She shrugged. "Your arteries. Tell me about it, Cliff."

"I can't tell you much. I'm mostly guessing. It looks as if Barnes became suspicious of Athena for some reason, did a bit of checking and investigating, and he really came up with something. The men in the photos are unloading a security van at night. They all look pretty edgy, and I'd say they're handling the proceeds of a robbery. As for the shotgun bits—seven shortened shotguns were used in a big payroll holdup earlier this year. It can't be a coincidence."

She stopped chewing her unsalted egg and unbuttered toast. "Athena Security men are armed robbers?"

"That's the way it looks."

"What about *her?*"

"It's hard to know what to think. O'Fear was very vague about where and when Barnes collected the stuff in the bag, and we've got no idea of the date of the photos, or of where they were taken."

"At the Athena place, surely?"

"Maybe. It looks as if Barnes sat on the evidence for a while. He was probably trying to work out what to do with it."

"Or trying to protect her."

I filed away sceptical, cynical, subversive thoughts of Barnes Todd the blackmailer. I was determined to get some breakfast and keep the temperature of the discussion low. I ate some more toast and egg and drank some coffee before I replied. "Or he could have been trying to find out whether she was involved. It's a big organisation. She might not know everything that goes on."

Felicia bit her lip and stared fiercely at the placid sea. "You're defending him and trying to shield her."

"Christ! I've never laid eyes on the woman."

Something in my tone alerted her. She swivelled around and stabbed the air with her fork. "I bet you have."

"Well, yes. I've seen her. But . . ."

"With Barnes?"

"Yes."

"Fuck you!"

"All I'm saying is that we're in the dark. Totally. We have to examine every possibility."

"I don't see why. We've got the evidence. Let's blow the whistle on them."

I shook my head. "It's not that easy. Photographs aren't much good as evidence. They can be faked and denied pretty easily."

"Especially if the photographer's dead?"

I nodded. "The stocks and barrels don't necessarily mean anything either. Not without O'Fear to testify as to where they came from and to identify the bag."

"Fingerprints?"

"Maybe."

"Where *is* O'Fear?"

"That's another thing I don't know." I ate the other egg and another piece of toast.

"I begin to get the idea," she said. "You've found out a lot of things, but you've still got more questions than answers. Is it always like this?"

I nodded. "Mostly. Sometimes it never becomes any clearer."

"That must be a bastard. Well, what d'you do next?"

"Investigate Athena and look for O'Fear."

"His name was the last sound Barnes uttered." Felicia's top lip trembled as she spoke, but she got it quickly under control. "That *has* to have some significance."

"You're right," I said, and left all the other things unsaid.

* * *

As we made the turn out of the national park, Felicia said, "I suppose you know you're screwing up my life?"

We had made love before leaving the house early in the afternoon. It hadn't been as good as the other times and we both knew it. We had both pretended otherwise, and we knew that too. I had the photographs in the glove box and the gar-bag on the back seat of the Falcon. I was thinking more about them and all the questions surrounding them than about the woman. That was part of the trouble.

"I'm sorry you feel like that, Fel. I wish you wouldn't."

"I suppose you think we'll end up just good friends when all this is over. Is this part of your investigative technique? Screwing one of the principals?"

I forced a laugh which sounded false, even to me. "I'm more likely to get screwed *by* the principals. Tell me, did you and Barnes talk much about him and Eleni Marinos?"

She was silent for a while, then she said, "Just once."

"Can you talk about it?"

She thought for about a mile before deciding she could talk. She told me that she'd found out that Barnes had spent a weekend at Thirroul with Eleni Marinos not long after their marriage. She had tackled him about it. "Barnes said it was to break off with her finally. I told him I thought our marriage was supposed to do that. He told me I didn't understand. Shit!"

She reached into the glove box for tissues; out of the corner of my eye I saw her hand fall on my gun in its holster. She was close to tears but she started to laugh instead. "Christ," she said. "A businessman who turns out to be a romantic and a tough guy who boils three-minute eggs. I can really pick 'em. My life's turning into a fantasy." She didn't cry, so she didn't need the tissue. She balled it up and threw it over her shoulder into the back seat with the gar-bag.

I reached across her and closed the glove box.

"Haven't you got a licence for it?" she said.

"I have. Let's stick to the point. Barnes must've said something more than, 'You don't understand.' He wasn't an inarticulate man."

"Sure. Sure. He said she'd helped him at a time when he needed help. She'd encouraged him when he needed encouragement. I wanted to hear that like I wanted to read my own obituary."

"That's all?"

"He said she was in a bad way now, and that there was nothing sexual between them. He couldn't just cut her off."

"What did he mean by that? Business or personal trouble?"

We were in Sydenham, negotiating the heavy traffic. I saw an Athena Security van up ahead and nearly braked as a reaction. She saw it too.

"I don't know," she said. "I'm beginning to think that these business types don't make a distinction. Like you."

"Come on, Fel. It's not like that."

"Isn't it? Well, anyway, I don't know whether it was the one or the other. I got in a rage and didn't listen."

"Try to remember. It could be important."

"Business. Personal. Who knows? There was a name mentioned. God, I don't know. Reagan? No, that's not it. Riley. Right. Riley was part of her trouble. Who the fuck's Riley?"

"He's in the picture," I said. "He owns trucks. And people."

All the oldtime pirates, bushrangers, and bank robbers thought the same—if you've got something to hide, they reckoned, stash it somewhere that's already been searched. Given that principle, I had plenty of hiding places available. I drove to Coogee, keeping a very careful watch for a tail. I circled the block around the Todd house, stopped, parked, and pulled out at irregular intervals. It was warm in the car, and the procedure was tedious.

"When can we stop this?" Felicia said.

I was doing a careful check of all the parked cars for a couple of blocks in each direction. I had three or four more streets to cover. "When I'm sure," I said.

"Wake me."

I went on with the tour and included the Coogee Bay hotel in the survey. A good pub to while away some time in, but I saw nothing suspicious. Finally I stopped outside the house. I opened the bag, put on my rubber gloves, and eased out two stocks and barrels. I wrapped a T-shirt lightly around them and put them with the photographs under the driver's seat. I put the plastic bag inside my overnight bag and zipped it. "Okay, Fel. Let's go inside." I knew what I wanted. I wanted to put the bag in her house and take her back to mine.

"You're going to walk into my house carrying your dirty weekend bag?"

"Has to be that way. I'm sorry. Are you worried about your reputation?"

She slung her own bag over her shoulder. "Who gives a shit?"

We went through the gate and up the path towards the house. "You haven't been back since the break-in, have you?" I pointed to the bushes by the verandah. "That's where I ripped my shirt getting up."

"Sue me," she said.

We went inside. Felicia prowled through the house, noting the results of the search—the disturbed rooms, the broken window in the kitchen. I gathered up the sheets she stripped savagely from the bed and put them on top of the gar-bag in the laundry basket that stood in the second bathroom beside the washer and dryer.

"Finished, have you?" She stood in the doorway, still holding her coat and looking at me as if I was the one who had desecrated her house.

I tugged at a sheet to give the laundry basket a natural look and didn't answer. The telephone rang and she grabbed it. She listened, sighed, and tapped her foot.

"All right," she said, and hung up.

I watched her as she paced the floor like a nervous parent. "Piers Lang," she said at last. "I gather you and he had a little talk?"

Her expression was fierce. I didn't reply.

"I can't stay here," she said. "I want to go to Redfern."

I looked at her. She was standing with her legs slightly apart as if balanced to throw a left hook. It wasn't the right time for me to offer her the comforts of my overpriced, undermaintained terrace. "That's a good idea. I'll drive you."

"I don't care whether you think it's a good idea or not. I'm going. My car's in the street. I'll drive myself. And you can go to hell."

I didn't argue. I left the house after getting the registration number of her white Camira and making sure she had my home and office numbers. I checked her car over carefully for signs of interference, found nothing, and drove off. I parked at the top of the street and waited until she left the house and got into the car. The Camira had stood idle for a good few days and she had some trouble starting it. I wondered if it would become a farce— me giving her a push. But the car started. She drove away fast and recklessly and I followed her, taking precautions. She parked in Chalmers Street and got out of the car, carrying her bag. She banged her knee and swore. Then she moved stiffly, tight with anger or sorrow or both. I would have liked to comfort her.

It was late in the day and I was tired. The embryonic beard was itchy on my face. I wanted a shower and a shave; I wanted a big drink and a house that didn't leak and smell of mould. I wanted a woman who didn't lie to me more than I lied to her and didn't change her mind and mood in ways I couldn't fathom. And I wanted to find Kevin O'Fearna.

22

I slept badly. I fancied I could hear burglars and arsonists and graffitists working their way through the house. I woke up a lot and had a few drinks. I finally got some sleep around dawn and felt like hell when I woke up at ten. The milk was sour and the bread was stale. I drank black coffee and scribbled notes in my notebook. Most of the notes ended in question marks. I went into the bathroom and looked at the beard. *Not too bad,* I thought. Bit of grey. Distinguished, intellectual even. Maybe if I kept it, I'd have some good ideas. I had a shower and began to feel better.

I drove in to Darlinghurst; the evidence I'd kept under the car seat and then under my bed I locked away in the office safe before I phoned Athena Security. The personnel manager was interested to hear from me. Yes, they were still recruiting. Yes, they valued experience. He only stopped saying yes when I said I'd need to talk to Eleni Marinos in person before I could consider joining the firm. He said he'd have to get back to me on that.

Call number two was to Michael Hickie. I asked him to find out all he could about Athena Security and its links, if any, to Riley's outfit.

"That's your line of territory," he said.

"I'll be working on it, too. I'll look into people and you can look into money."

"I'm interested in people too, you know."

"Don't be," I said. "Most aren't worth the trouble."

"You're low. Having trouble with Felicia?"

I grunted.

"Barnes said she was trouble, but worth it."

I grunted again and hung up. I'd had to quote the number on my operator's licence to the Athena bloke and, in the process of locating it, I had strewn the contents of my wallet across the desk. I looked at the credit cards and the meagre amount of cash and the creased driver's licence and suddenly felt small and isolated. My only backup in the office was an answering machine; my only means of transport was the Falcon; I had an illegal Colt .45 and a properly licenced Smith & Wesson .38 for firepower. No helicopters, no armoured vans, no shotguns. Who was I kidding? This was too big for me.

It was midday and I was dry. Well, that's what a cask of red wine is for. I poured a small one, swallowed it along with some pride, and phoned Detective-Inspector Frank Parker of the New South Wales Police, a body whose motto is, "Punishment swiftly follows the crime." Two years ago Parker had married Hilde Stoner, who had been a lodger in my house. They now had a son whom they had named after me.

"Parker."

"Hardy."

"Gidday, Cliff. How many favours can I do you? Just ask."

"Christ, what's got into you? Did your shares go up?"

"What shares? No, your namesake took his first steps last night."

"Bit slow off the mark, isn't he?"

"Piss off. Twelve months. Bit above average."

"That'd be right. Hilde okay? Good. Look, Frank, I've got a bit of a problem." I kept it vague, but intimated that I might have evidence connected with a major crime or possibly a series of crimes. I don't why I said that, probably because cops say it.

"I hear you went bail for O'Fear," Frank said. "Is there a connection?"

"Could be. Are your people still interested in fingerprints and microscopic fibres and that sort of thing? Or do you just wait for the crims to blow each other away these days?"

"Spare me the mordant wit, Cliff. What do you want?"

"A talk. After work today, in the bar at Central Railway?"

"Are you catching a train somewhere?"

"No, I like the atmosphere."

"Are you okay, Cliff?"

"Is anyone? See you around six, Frank."

I had some more wine, which I sipped slowly while I looked out at the blue sky through the grey-brown window. I plucked at my near-beard but didn't feel any brighter. I poured another glass of wine, and when the phone rang I reached for it, lazily, thinking it would be the man from Athena. I lifted the receiver and two men walked into the office without knocking. One of them was big and one was small. The small one held a gun that looked like a .357 Magnum Colt, the one with the short barrel. It made him seem a lot bigger than he was. He gestured with the Colt for me to hand the phone to the big man. I didn't do it, so the big man punched me in the face. I dropped the phone as I rocked back in my chair. He picked it up from the desk.

"Right," he said into the receiver. "We're here." He replaced the receiver and sat down in the hard, unpadded client's chair. The lack of comfort didn't seem to bother him. The small man leaned against the wall beside the half-open door; he held the gun in such a way that a ten-centimetre movement would train it on my chest.

"I think it's time we stopped pissing around, Hardy," the big man said. "I'm Stanley Riley."

I rubbed my cheekbone where the punch had landed. He had pulled it so that the skin hadn't split and I'd been more surprised than hurt. Expert stuff. He was well over six feet tall and beefy with it, although his well-cut grey suit concealed the flab. His face had that plain, fleshy, stamped-out-of-the-mould look you see on prison guards and ex-footballers. He had heavy eyebrows and a deep dimple in his chin that wasn't cute. His mouth was a thin, hard split in the lower end of his face and his eyes were wide apart, bland and innocent.

I pointed to the gunman. "And what's his name?"

"He doesn't matter."

"Hear that?" I said. "You don't matter."

The gunman had a dark wispy beard, a walleye and a scarred, puckered left cheek. He looked through me towards the window but it was hard to tell where he was really looking. He reached out and put the Colt on top of my filing cabinet. Then he reached into the pocket of his windbreaker and took out a single cigarette. He lit it with a disposable lighter, blew smoke, and reclaimed his gun. He didn't speak.

I picked up my Vegemite glass and drank some wine.

"A cheap private investigator," Riley said. "Drinking cheap plonk."

"Cask wine and French brandy," I said. "The effect's the same. What's on your mind, Stan?"

"You are. I'm wondering how to stop you causing me any trouble."

"Now how could I cause you trouble? A cheap . . ."

"You've been phoning around. Trying to set up a meeting

with Marinos, poking into my business affairs and talking to the police. I'm worried."

"You've been listening in. That's illegal."

"Everything's illegal these days, Hardy. A while ago I could've just neutralised you—got your licence cancelled, got you a few months on remand, bored it up you. But with this new mob coming into government . . . it takes time to make the right contacts."

"Psychic, are you? The election's a week away."

"It's in the bag."

"I must get a bet on," I said. I had the Vegemite glass and could reach the telephone. Not very potent weapons. The .357 Colt would make a lot of noise but there weren't many people in the building to hear it, and probably none who would care.

"You've really been poking around, Hardy. You mentioned fingerprints and fibres. I reckon you've got the bits of the shot-guns."

I didn't say anything, tried to keep my face neutral.

"Gary here got careless," Riley said. "That's why I brought him along. He's itching for a chance to make up for his mis-take."

"You've made a lot of mistakes, Stan."

"Well, I'll just have to set things right, won't I? Starting with you. The shotguns're ashes and lumps of metal now, all except for the bits you've got."

"There's some photographs too. I don't know how many cop-ies."

Riley plucked at the hole in his big chin. He must have found it hard to shave there and a couple of bristles were annoying him. "I'm not too worried about photographs. I might do a deal on the negatives if you've got them."

"Deal?"

"You don't think I want to strong-arm you, do you? I'm a

businessman. I find all this stuff very distasteful, and I want to put an end to it. That's why I'm here."

Gary sniffed. He dropped his butt on the floor and stepped on it. Then he used his free hand to scratch his crotch. Talk evidently bored him. He saw me watching him and turned his head slightly to bring me into his strange field of vision. He was small, but not as small as the man who had followed me and run up against O'Fear. That one had excelled at evasion; this one looked as if he liked to see blood flowing. Riley reached into his pocket and took out a chequebook.

"What're you being paid on this job?"

"Ten thousand dollars."

He nodded, reached out, and picked up a ballpoint pen from my desk. He blew on it to get rid of the dust and made a few trial scratches on the cover of the chequebook. On the fourth scratch the pen worked. "I'll double it."

"No sale," I said.

He sighed. "I thought it might be like that. A man of integrity, eh? Too bad."

"And curiosity," I said. "Tell me a bit about it. We might be able to reach an arrangement."

Riley examined my face for what seemed like five minutes but was probably thirty seconds. Time frames change when the pressure comes on. I stared back at him and tried to guess his age and background. About fifty, I decided. School of hard knocks, with an overlay of sophistication picked up late. Possibly from a woman. He fiddled with the pen, flexed it between his thick fingers, and snapped it like a matchstick. He seemed like a man who had followed his instincts for most of his life but had recently got smarter and learned to use his brains. Under stress, though, it was a struggle between the two approaches. Gary yawned and lit another cigarette.

"Okay," Riley said. "I'll put you in the picture. Todd was

doing pretty well, competing with me for hauling and storing. He had better people working for him."

"He was a leader of men," I said. "Were you ever in the army?"

Riley flushed. "No. I tried to buy him out and he wouldn't agree. Then he got shitty about security. Started to look into that end of the business."

This was quite a lot of talk. I thought if I could keep it going, Gary might nod off. "There's a whole set of photographs," I said. "They show security fuck-ups—guards asleep, patrols not checking gates, boozing on the job. Like that."

Riley was sharp-witted and shrewd. "You're guessing."

I shrugged.

"Doesn't matter," he said. "He got interested in security and he got interested in Eleni. I didn't like that."

"Which?"

"Both."

"How does she fit into all this? Does she know about the hold-ups and all the rest of it?"

"I think we're getting off the point."

"Why did you kill Barnes?"

"He was careless. He had something he shouldn't have had, and he tried to use it against me."

"To what end?"

"He wanted in on the operation."

I shook my head. "That's bullshit, Riley. Todd passed up a dozen opportunities for dirty money. It was the woman, wasn't it?"

"You didn't know the bastard. He wanted her *and* the action. He thought I was just a dumb mick. He was wrong."

"Are you trying to tell me you protected Eleni Marinos from Todd?"

It was a crucial question but it really didn't make any difference. *Poor Felicia,* I thought.

Riley was all bluster now. "I've said enough, and you've said fuck all. It's time for you to give a bit, Hardy. What've you got to sell?"

Gary had disposed of his second butt in the same way and was looking more interested in the proceedings. Riley was an impatient and insecure man. My references to Eleni Marinos had touched him in a vulnerable place and tipped the scales against me. The door was standing half open. I wondered whether I had any chance of getting past Gary and out. Not much, certainly not from where I sat. I opened a drawer in the desk and looked up to see the Colt pointing at my Adam's apple. I moved slowly and showed Riley the safe key. He nodded and I got up, moved around the desk, and squatted in front of the safe. The open door was a metre and a half away, and Gary glided smoothly into place to block it off. Neat.

I opened the safe and lifted out the barrels and stocks, using the rubber gloves like potholders. Riley motioned for me to put them on the desk. He gave Gary a look that came from his past. "You fuckin' idiot," he said.

"Where's the rest of them, cunt?" Gary said.

I went back behind the desk and didn't answer. Riley got up from his chair and felt around in the safe. There was only one other thing to find—the photographs. He took out the envelope and slopped them onto the desk. The glossy pictures sat on top of the scratched bits of wood and metal.

Riley looked at them, moved a couple aside for a better appraisal, and shook his head slowly. "Fuckin' Todd," he said. "Why couldn't he be smart?" The smoothness was gone from him now. It was almost as if the smell of the wharves or the trucks or the mines had settled back over him, expensive suit and all. He struggled for control, clicked his tongue, and settled down in his chair. "Hardy, I want it all."

"Why don't we have a drink?" I reached for the cask. Two litres of rough red against a .357 Colt.

"Put it down," Gary said.

Maybe he didn't mean to do it, maybe it was the old, instinctive Riley acting, but he took his chequebook from the desk and put it back in his pocket. I felt a chill run through me. Suddenly I was back in Malaya, feeling cold, although the temperature was in the nineties and I was sweating. The two Chinese soldiers were running at me, screaming their lungs out, and I didn't know how many rounds I had left in the Sten gun . . .

Riley rubbed the back of his head; the carefully cut grey hair stood up at the crown. "We're still talking. You've put the rest of the stuff somewhere."

"Somewhere," I said. "But you've put your money away, Stan. That wasn't subtle. If I tell you what you want to know, I'm dead."

"You could be persuaded to tell. I didn't want this to get messy, but I could give you to Gary."

I shook my head. "If you give me to Gary he'd have to use his gun. I know a bit about guns. He's got a good one there, but I might get to him. If I did, I'd put his eyes out."

"Try it," Gary said.

"Wait on." Riley looked at me so hard I could feel the force of it on my face. I wanted to put my hand up, to block out his gaze, but I resisted the impulse. His thin, sharklike lips parted. "Mrs. Todd," he said slowly. "That's the key. D'you know anyone who lives in Chalmers Street, Redfern? Apart from Mrs. Todd, I mean?"

I didn't answer.

"Pity," Riley said, "if you did, you could call 'em up and ask if there's one of my trucks in the street and an Athena van by the park."

"She doesn't know a thing," I said.

"I think she does. I think she knows all we need to know. I can see it in your fuckin' face under that stupid beard." He swayed a little to the left, away from where the gunman stood. "Gary, we don't need him any more."

Gary's hand moved and I started to move too, up and to one side, as if he was the conductor and I was a violinist in an orchestra. I knew I'd be way too slow but it was better than just sitting there waiting for the bullets. My eyes were closed: I felt the explosion bounce off the walls and floor and ceiling, and fill the room with echoing sound.

23

The second explosion came only a split second later, but in that time I recorded a few impressions. I wasn't shot; someone had come into the room from the passage; Gary had been thrown around like a soft toy . . . My movement in reaction to Gary's with the Colt had taken me over to the wall by the window. At the second blast the window shattered and I was showered with glass. I dropped to the floor and found Stanley Riley down there. He was writhing and cursing; there was a gaping hole in the floorboards and the worn old carpet square around it was scorched and sticky with blood.

A sharp sound made me look up. O'Fear had worked the pump action and was pointing a shotgun at Riley's head.

"O'Fear, don't!" I scrambled to my feet and moved towards him. He held the gun very steady as if he was taking aim, although at that range he couldn't miss. Riley had guts; he looked at me and then at his legs. His grey trousers had turned black and there were puddles of blood around his knees and ankles. Blood was dripping into his shoes.

"Get an ambulance." He ground the words out and clenched his jaw tightly as he struggled to get into a sitting position by the wall. O'Fear tracked him with the gun, but the murderous impulse had passed. He took his finger off the trigger as I grabbed for the phone. I called for an ambulance and also rang Frank Parker. When I put the phone down, I discovered that my recently healed hand was bloody from nicks and scratches caused by the broken glass. So we had the unwounded, the slightly wounded, the seriously wounded, and the dead, all in one room.

Gary lay on his back in front of the safe. The charge had taken him in the left side below the armpit. Splintered rib bones stuck out through the bloody red meat and grey lung tissue. His eyes were open and bulging, and blood trickled from his nose and mouth.

A white, startled face appeared in the door. The iridologist. "All under control," I croaked. I waved her away with my bloody paw and she went. O'Fear put the shotgun on the desk and looked at the spread of photographs. He glanced at Riley, who was sitting with his back against the wall and his eyes closed. For a moment I thought O'Fear was going to pick up the gun and I got ready to stop him, but he relaxed and pointed to the photographs.

"See," he said. His breath was whisky-laden, and there was a hysterical note in his voice.

"What?"

O'Fear's finger pointed to one of the men wearing a silver jacket and carrying a rifle. The face was sharp in every detail— the loose, slack mouth, the guileless eyes, and soft jawline. It was the face I knew I'd seen but couldn't put a name to.

"That's Danny," O'Fear said. "My boy. These bastards have got him into the sort of trouble he'll never . . ." He closed his eyes and struck himself on the chest with his fist. "They killed a guard, didn't they? Danny'll die in gaol."

"Easy," I said. "He mightn't have been involved."

"He was. You've just got a few of the pictures here. I found a lot more in the office. Danny's in them all. Bastards! He can barely write his own name, y'know. But there's no real harm in him, if he's left alone."

"So what've you been doing?"

"I went looking for Danny, a'course, but I couldn't get to him. He's holed up in that bloody Athena fortress, I suspect. I was coming to see you here when I saw a couple of them in those poncy silver jackets using a scanner outside. Then these two arrived. I got hold of this pump gun the other day. I brought it with me and sneaked up for a listen. I heard enough."

"I have to thank you," I said. "He was going to shoot me. I'll say that loud and clear to every cop and lawyer I meet. You'll be all right."

He nodded. Riley groaned and swore. "Where's that bloody ambulance?"

"Did you have to shoot him?" I said.

"I didn't shoot him. I wanted to, but I pulled down and fired it into the floor. He'll live. Y'don't think it'd be a good idea for me to scarper?"

"I do not," I said.

The ambulance men came, and the cops came, and there was a lot of standing around and photographing and measuring and collecting of trophies. I was treated for my cuts and Riley got some temporary relief for his pain and discomfort. Frank Parker put in an appearance. He was careful not to interfere with the work of the detectives from the Kings Cross station, but I managed to tell him that a few cruising squad cars along Chalmers Street, Redfern, could be useful. Riley refused to make a statement without his lawyer being present. O'Fear and I made statements and the photographs and shotgun parts made a big impression. Still, cops are cops.

Detective Sergeant Blazey looked at his notes. "I can't count the number of bail provisions you're in violation of, O'Fear."

The ambulance men spread heavy plastic over a stretcher, lifted Gary's body aboard, and carried him out.

"He was acting as my operative," I said. "That should give him some protection."

Blazey, a dark good-looking man in a good-looking suit, lit a cigarette with a gold lighter. "Don't make me laugh. Christ, this place is a mess." He consulted his notes again. "Two shots. What happened to the window?"

"The building's old," I said. "It probably just couldn't stand the pressure. Like me."

Blazey blew smoke. "Now I'm going to cry. You should've come to us the minute you got hold of this stuff, Hardy."

"I know I could have come to you, Sergeant. I know you're a man of integrity. But we've only just met. I think Riley owns a few of your colleagues, if you'll excuse me saying so. I was working my way towards the police."

"Through Parker?"

I nodded.

Blazey gave the all-clear for the ambulance men to put Riley on a stretcher. "Parker's okay," he said. He pointed his cigarette at O'Fear. "Gary Gilbert's an escapee and no bloody loss. That's lucky for you."

"Getting a break on that holdup and killing's going to be very lucky for you, Sergeant," O'Fear said. "What about my boy?"

Blazey turned away. O'Fear reached out and grabbed his well-cut sleeve. "What about Danny?"

Blazey's civilised veneer cracked. "Take your fuckin' hand off me. You're charged with manslaughter. Like father, like son. Your kid'll be lucky if he's not up for murder."

O'Fear punched him; Blazey reeled back with blood spurting from his nose down the front of his immaculate shirt and jacket. One of the uniformed men, a lightly built, fresh-faced youngster, tried to grab O'Fear from behind. He didn't have a chance; O'Fear fought him off. He bullocked his way to the desk and grabbed the shotgun.

"Bugger you all!" he bellowed. "Bastards!" He worked the pump action and swung the gun towards us—Blazey, two uniformed men, a forensic guy, and me.

I jumped towards him with my hands outstretched to beat down the gun. I yelled, "O'Fear! No!"

I felt the heat of the bullet that missed me by millimetres, hit O'Fear above the right eye, and sprayed his brains and blood all over me.

24

Gary Gilbert's fingerprints were all over the stocks and barrels of the shotguns, but Gary Gilbert was dead. O'Fear was dead, too, and without him to identify where the evidence had come from, the case against Riley and Athena was cloudy. I didn't know how hard they searched or where, but no trace of the other photographs O'Fear referred to could be found. The few I had, with no negatives, and without Riley in them, didn't carry much weight. I had no witnesses to support my claim that Riley had threatened my life, and Blazey was adamant that the uniformed man who had shot O'Fear had prevented a massacre.

"You know, it's funny," I said to Parker several days later, "it's almost as if Gilbert and O'Fear shot each other. A sort of criminal shootout. One of the papers wrote it up like that."

"Yeah, I saw it," Parker said. "The journos are getting younger and dumber every day. Eleni Marinos is out of the country. Did you know that?"

"Doesn't surprise me. How does it look for Riley?"

We were in a pub in William Street, surrounded by New Zealanders who were having a celebration—half of them were dark-skinned with crinkly hair and broad noses, so it couldn't have been for winning the Maori land wars. They whooped and hollered and I had to lean close to hear what Parker said.

"Prosecutor's having trouble finding the right charge. They might get him on tax."

"Tax? Shit! The bastard masterminded armed hold-ups. A man was killed."

Parker shrugged. "He's got lawyers with more letters after their names than it takes to spell yours."

"They'll find a scapegoat."

Parker sighed. "Maybe."

"He's got cops in his pocket, Frank."

"Probably. All that's changing, Cliff. But it takes time."

I drank some beer and didn't say any of the things that were on my mind. It wasn't Parker's fault that the police force was corrupt. He had run up against it himself a few years back and had nearly been steamrolled. And he was right; it was changing slowly, very slowly, imperceptibly even. It wasn't my fault that Barnes Todd had deceived everybody, and who was I to go around shattering illusions? I thought about Bob Mulholland and Felicia and the way we construct things to suit us.

Parker and I drank and chatted about this and that—Hilde and his son, his prospects for promotion, my move to Bondi.

"You'll never do it," Parker said. "No, you might. If there's a woman in the picture. Is there?"

I said I didn't know, which was the truth. I hadn't seen Felicia since I'd followed her to Redfern. Since then, all communication had been through Michael Hickie. Frank and I finished our drinks and left the pub as the Enzedders were going into a *haka*. We agreed to play tennis sometime soon. I walked up William Street towards the Cross. The days were starting out bright, warming up briefly, and then getting cool, the way it happens in

March. A bus belched diesel fumes over me and I coughed and spluttered all the rest of the way to Darlinghurst.

Riley had been right about the election result—it had been out with the old and in with the new, with a vengeance. Maybe it was time to join the politicians, who would be selling houses in electorates they no longer represented and moving out of offices they no longer needed. When I had left an hour or so earlier, I was seriously contemplating the move to Bondi. My office was a wreck and I had moved into an empty one down the hall without asking anyone's permission. I quite liked it; it had a better view. But it felt very temporary. Turning into St. Peter's Lane, I was surprised to see scaffolding being erected around the building and extension ladders in place. A gang of men in painter's overalls were unloading their gear from a van.

"What's going on?" I asked one of them.

"Bit of a paint job, mate."

"I heard they were going to tear the place down."

He scratched his head and squinted up at the building. It was solid but undistinguished, no candidate for a National Trust order. "It's happening all over the place," he said. "They've done their dough on the stock market and have to hang on to what they've got. It's work for us, we're not complaining."

"What colour's it going to be?"

"Cream with brown trim."

"Very nice."

Inside the building were men working on the stairs and wiring. They told me the same story—repairs, not refitting. It was all very comforting. I went up to my new office, shifted the furniture around, and stuck a clean card onto the door with a new drawing pin.

Two nights later I met Felicia Todd and Michael Hickie, by appointment, in a Glebe restaurant called the Melting Pot. It's the sort of place where you have to beat a path through thick fernery and politeness, but the food's good. I arrived first and was halfway through a light beer when they joined me. Felicia had done something different with her hair and was wearing very high heels and an elegant blouse and skirt. Hickie's suit was new-looking and his shirt was very white. I felt down-at-heel in my cord jacket and faded denim shirt. I had trimmed my beard, though, and I thought it gave me an international look.

"Hello, hello," I said. "Push a few fronds aside and sit down."

They sat, and the drink waiter rushed up to take Felicia's order for dry sherry and Hickie's for a martini. I drained my beer and asked for another. The waiter reached for my glass but I held onto it. "Bring the can," I said. "I like this glass."

We looked at the menu while we waited for the drinks. When they came my beer was in a fresh glass, and the waiter deftly removed the old one.

"Waiter—one, customer—nil," I said.

Hickie took an envelope from his breast pocket and passed it across. "Ten thousand dollars," he said. The envelope looked small in his big hand; the smart tailoring didn't conceal the strength in his shoulders, and there was a new confidence in his voice.

"Thanks," I said. Now that O'Fear was dead it was all mine. I could buy some tax-protected bonds, or go to Europe for a month, or get my bathroom fixed.

"You don't look too happy," Hickie said.

I drank some beer. "Did you do what I asked you?"

I had given Hickie a list of the dates of some of the biggest armed hold-ups over the past two years and asked him to try to relate these to developments within the Athena organisation—hiring, equipment buying, expansions. He sipped his martini and looked around. His expression was relaxed. When his eye fell on Felicia's long, firm neck and square shoulders, flattered by her silk blouse, he smiled appreciatively. "I had a shot at it. It was a pretty tall order, but I made some calls and did the best I could."

"And?" I said.

"You could be right. They seem to have had surges of cash flow. Riley owns forty-nine per cent, by the way."

"Does Eleni Marinos own the rest?"

Hickie shot an uneasy glance at Felicia, who still hadn't said a word other than to order her drink. "Maybe. It's hard to say. She's a mystery woman."

Felicia closed her menu with a snap. "Who cares? Everybody involved in security's a crook, it's well known. Michael's going to run Barnes Enterprises, but there's not going to be a security division, is there, Michael? Marinos and Riley can steal as much as they like. Who cares?"

"What are you going to do, Fel?" I said.

She stared at me, defying me to offer a syllable or gesture of contradiction. "I'm going to organise Barnes' exhibition. I'm going to write the catalogue. I'm going to set up and administer an artist's scholarship with some of the money."

Hickie nodded and finished his drink.

"Then what?" I said.

She picked up her sherry and took a sip. She was carefully made up and was very close to being beautiful. But there was something wrong with her, some deeper level of disturbance I couldn't fathom. "The police came to my house and got those horrible things you left there," she said slowly.

"I would've warned you, but I thought you were in Redfern."

"Doesn't matter. They must've thought I had something to do with it, because one of them said he'd keep me out of trouble if I'd fuck him."

Hickie put his hand over hers.

"I mentioned your name and he laughed. He left me alone, but he said he hoped I was fucking you good because you were on borrowed time."

"I'm sorry," I said. "I really am. That must've been terrible for you, but it doesn't mean anything. It's just dumb, macho cop talk."

Hickie put his arm around her shoulders. "Felicia and I are getting married," he said.

The day of O'Fear's funeral was like midwinter. The rain began at dawn and didn't let up. The sky remained a dull grey with dark, low clouds, and there was a wind that drove the rain into your face. I got wet running from the front door to the car; my shoes leaked and water trickled from my hair down the back of my neck. It was a miserable drive to the Catholic church, where the officiating person had trouble pronouncing O'Fear's name, and a damp, dreary procession to the cemetery.

Mourners were few. I recognised two of O'Fear's drinking mates and a couple of unionists. An Irishman who used to play in a bush band with O'Fear was there. He was weeping, drunk already. There were no women. We stood beside the hole in the ground and the cheap box, while the priest mumbled; someone held an umbrella over him, but the rain still managed to streak the pages of his gilt-edged Bible. I wasn't feeling much. A headache set up by a fair bit of drinking the night before had wiped out some sensitivity; my wet feet took some of my attention. I was nagged by an irrational thought that they were putting O'Fear in a wet hole, like planting a shrub.

I heard a loud sniff and looked in the direction it came from. Three men stood tightly bunched; the one in the middle was crying. He was Danny O'Fearna. When the muddy earth was being shovelled into the hole, I went across to Danny.

"I'm Cliff Hardy," I said. "A friend of your Dad's."

He moved as if to put out his hand to shake, but stopped, and I saw that he was handcuffed to the man next to him.

"What's this?" I said.

His face was wet from rain and tears, and his loose foolish mouth had trouble forming the words. "They're doin' me for armed hold-up."

"You and how many others?"

"Just me," Danny said.

The cop jerked his wrist sharply; O'Fearna yelped and they took him away.

I drank some rum for medicinal reasons on the drive home. The rain eased and had stopped by the time I turned into Glebe Point Road. The sky to the west had split open, and blue and white patches were expanding, spreading, and bursting out in all directions. A beam of sunlight slanted through the tall poplars and filled the car with a pale green light. When I got out in front of my house I could taste the cleanness of the rainswept air. The tin roof of the house on the other side of the street was glinting in the sun and steam rose from it in little spurts. I walked down the narrow space beside the house and the fence and felt the overgrown bushes and vines drip on me. What the hell, I was wet already.

I stood on the bricks Hilde had laid in the pocket-sized back-yard and looked at the pot plants Helen had left behind. She used to water them regularly and pick off the bugs; since she left the plants have experienced only droughts and flooding rains. I stood on a pile of newspapers and looked over the back fence between the flats to Blackwattle Bay. Up close the water would be murky, but from here it was a deep green. Who needs the Pacific Ocean when you've got Blackwattle Bay?

A scratching sound made me turn sharply. I remembered Felicia's cop's remark about being on borrowed time. I was wet, full of rum and nostalgia, and unarmed. Prime time.

The cat scrambled down from the roof where it had been clawing, probably at a bird's nest, and ambled across to rub itself against my leg.

"Jesus," I said. "What happened to you?" It was favouring

one leg and had angry, encrusted wounds on its head. It rubbed and purred. "I suppose you're telling me I should see the other guy. Anyway, welcome back to bachelorland."

It left me and hopped across the bricks to the corner of the lean-to. The fibro had sagged away from the studs, and the cat probed the gap with its paw.

"Forget it. I'll open the door." The cat mewed and clawed. "If it's a mouse," I said, "go for it."

The cat scratched and something fell from the wall cavity. I went over and picked it up. It was a thick manila envelope, heavily wrapped in polythene and sealed with insulating tape. I opened the back door and let the cat run past me. It stood mewing in the kitchen while I opened the envelope.

Inside were about fifty of Barnes Todd's photographs: the collection included those I had seen, and a whole lot more. Stan Riley's face was unmistakable as he apparently supervised the transshipment of sealed security bags from an Athena van to a Riley truck. Also in the envelope was a thick wad of negatives.

The cat screeched and tried to lift the lino with its claws. I put some stale cereal, old ham slices, and dried-out tuna in a bowl, and it looked at me reproachfully.

"I'll get you the best," I said. "Later."

It was pretty clear what Barnes had done. He had taken the shots showing Danny O'Fearna from the bunch, probably to enlist O'Fear's help in some sort of blackmail operation. Well, he had overreached himself. But I was left with a question that had been working its way steadily forward in my head since the image of Barnes Todd first began to lose its shine. The question could have only one answer. I reached for the phone and dialled Hickie's number.

"I'll put you through, Mr. Hardy," Jenny said.

Hickie came on the line and I told him about finding the photographs. I also told him about the incident in Korea and Todd's continuing relationship with Eleni Marinos.

Hickie said nothing.

"He was only fair as an artist," I said. "The real talent's in Felicia's photography. Did you know that?"

"I had a pretty good idea," Hickie said. "So what's your point, Hardy?"

"Todd had too much to hide to invite someone like me to sniff around his affairs."

"Right," Hickie said.

"You forged the note. You wanted Felicia and the business, but you wanted to know exactly what was involved. You wanted to come into money, but not into trouble."

"It takes one battler to understand another," Hickie said.

"Took a chance, didn't you, Michael? What if Felicia and I had stuck?"

Hickie laughed. "I didn't take much of a chance. I checked on you first—you and women and your impossible way of life. I knew you'd screw it up. You always have."

"You and Todd were a good pair," I said.

"That's another thing—Felicia needs someone who thinks Barnes Todd was a saint on wheels, and I fill the bill. I knew it'd all come right. Just happened a bit quicker than I expected."

"I wonder you didn't try to con me out of the ten thousand."

"I thought about it, but I couldn't figure a way. No hard feelings, eh, Cliff?"

I think we hung up at the same time.

O'Fear's hiding place had been pretty smart—who looks in the walls of bathrooms for anything but white ants? I took the photos and put them down beside the phone. You can never tell the whole story; the thing is to tell the parts that matter. I thought about Danny O'Fearna and his sorry, bewildered face. I took the .45 from the cupboard and put it on top of the photos. I thought about Riley and Athena and about bugs and scanners.

To hell with it, they think they're in the clear. I dialled Frank Parker's number.

"Parker."

"This is Hardy, Frank. What about a game of squash when you knock off?"

"You hate squash."

"I've learned a few shots I'd like to show you."

About the Author

Peter Corris was born in Stawell, Victoria, in 1942. He has worked as a lecturer and researcher in history, as well as a freelance writer and journalist, specialising in sports writing. He has written thrillers, a social history of prizefighting in Australia, quiz books, radio and television scripts, and the historical novel *The Gulliver Fortune*. *O'Fear* is the twelfth in his series of books about Sydney-based private eye Cliff Hardy.